LEVIN'S MILL

LEVIN'S MILL

Johannes Bobrowski

Translated from the German by Janet Cropper

A NEW DIRECTIONS BOOK

Originally published in 1964 by Union Verlag—VOB—Berlin/GDR as
Levins Mühle.
Published by arrangement with Marion Boyars Publishers
Manufactured in the United States of America.
New Directions Books are printed on acid-free paper.
Published simultaneously in Canada by Penguin Books Canada Limited.

Library of Congress Cataloging-in-Publication Data

Bobrowski, Johannes, 1917-1965
    [Levin's Mühle. English]
    Levin's mill / Johannes Bobrowski ; translated by Janet Cropper.
        p.   cm.
    ISBN 0-8112-1315-3 (alk. paper)
    I. Cropper, Janet   II. Title
    PT2603.013L413   1996
    833'.914—dc20   95-47598
                                            CIP

Celebrating 60 years of publishing for James Laughlin
by New Directions Publishing Corporation
80 Eighth Avenue, New York 10011

LEVIN'S MILL

CHAPTER ONE

Perhaps it's unfair of me to tell you the story of how my grandfather swept away the mill, and then again, perhaps it's not unfair. Even if it does have consequences for the family. Whether something is right and proper or not depends on where you are—but where am I?—and to tell a story you must simply make a start. I think it's wrong if you know in advance exactly what you want to say and how long it's going to take. At any rate it doesn't get you anywhere. You must make a start, and naturally you know where you are going to start, you know that all right but that's about all, just the first sentence, that's still a problem. Well then, the first sentence.

The Drewenz is a tributary in Poland.

There's the first sentence and right away I hear you say: so your grandfather was a Pole. And I reply: no he wasn't. And so, as you see, there's already room for mistakes and that's a poor start. Well then, a new first sentence.

In the 1870's on the lower reaches of the Vistula, on one of its minor tributaries, there was a village populated predominantly by Germans.

All right, that's the first sentence. But you would have to add that it was a flourishing village with huge barns and solid sheds, and that many farmyards there, I mean the actual yards—the areas between the house and barn, cowshed, stable and cellar and attic—were half the size of some entire villages in other districts. And I should have to say that the stoutest farmers were Germans, the Poles in the village were poorer though certainly not so poor as in the outlying Polish timber villages. But I won't say that, I'll say instead that the Germans were called Kaminski, Tomaschewski and Korsakowski and the Poles Lebrecht and Germann. And that's the way it really was.

Now I must convince you that the story should be told because it's right and proper to tell it and family considerations play no part. I said before that whether it is right and proper or not depends on where I am, so I must establish that first and then get on and tell the story, otherwise you can't form an opinion about it.

People like to have firm opinions and perhaps it's all the same to some of them where they collect the opinions, but it's not the same to me, and that's why I'm going to tell the story. People who don't mind how their opinions are formed will maintain that clear vision should not be clouded by a particular knowledge of the facts and they do have a point, art for example, would not be as blithe as Schiller has it, without this principle; however, we prefer to make use of our knowledge of the facts and be accurate, in other words cloud our clear vision.

> Clouded, clouded, ever clouded,
> Never shall the sun break through,

as the reverend Feller, Champion of the Faith, would have sung, but that's looking too far ahead. Now we'll fish around in these troubled waters, we don't want to look too far ahead, but we catch something which suits us very well—there are a couple of figures of whom at least one looks every bit as fine as we, but there are bound to be a few more.

I am sitting—and this is the answer to the question 'where am I?'—a couple of hundred miles as the crow flies, to the west of that village on the Vistula. I don't know if the village

6

still exists; it doesn't matter, the people who lived then don't exist any more, just us, grand-children and great-grand-children. Maybe it's utterly futile to tell the whole story now, just as futile as if I had dished it up then to my grandfather, afterwards when he was in Briesen and still had enough to live on as an old man, sitting there in three rooms and a kitchen alone with his wife, having quarrelled with his children, who, in turn, also had enough to live on and were busy quarrelling with the grand-children. Quite successfully, I know. And here, at the close of the introduction, which ended with the intimation of a fear that I hope will be groundless, the action of the story begins. The second sentence as it were. On the right the Voice of Faith, on the left the Gospel Song-ster, two black books, bound in black calico, well preserved, just a metre above the sandy path. All this is clearly visible, although the handsome books are being swung to and fro by an absurdly lanky man, holding them in his absurdly lanky arms. A sombre man with a tiny head on which is perched a sombre black hat. But what would this head be without the long, black, drooping moustaches, tailing off in two smooth, stiff strands, this small, narrow head with the slanting eyes, this pallid face reminiscent of sour milk. The reverend Feller is walking up the footpath from the main road, where the sheep come in the evening when the swallows soar windward for the last flight of the day, but now it's morning, late morn-ing, the hour which brings the swallows out for one last brief flight before the noonday heat sets in.

The house seems to be locked, but is in fact open. Go round the garden and through the entrance near the locked yard-gate and the following sight meets your eyes: the front door of the house is open and on the threshhold Glinski, the gander, is standing and surveying his approaching enemy. Feller has caught sight of him too and, in sheer determination, is chang-

7

ing over the Voice of Faith into his left hand to join the Gospel Songster, in order to have his right hand free. He's a fighter and will beat this satan incarnate, this **Glinski,** he'll force his entry into the house, he doesn't even need a stick, just a smattering of Polish. Glinski, a German gander, can't stand that, any more than the real Glinski, the preacher at Malken who always bellows so loudly.

There is the old devil. Squawking away to himself uneasily. One more step Feller, then Glinski will sound his trumpet-call and up will go the hind-quarters of the wild ram behind the barn, and, head lowered, weight on his spindly forelegs, he'll charge first the fence and then the wall of the barn and the turkeys will rush round the end of the stable into the yard, wings pressed to the ground, rattling like chain-mail, gobbling their whole cacophonous range of screeches like steam-organs at full pressure.

I'm coming in, you Devil you, says Feller darkly, in Polish and has taken the aforementioned single step, this Champion of the Faith, but now he comes to a halt as Glinski is reacting all wrongly. The trumpet blast came, so far, so good, the turkey-cocks are there, the whole fighting force is lined up in the middle of the yard in front of the empty rack-wagon and blasts of noise are coming at regular intervals from behind the barn as Mahlke, the old ram, always takes his fifteen steps backwards before battering his skull against the wall again. But now Glinski ought to be stretching out his neck, his head almost touching the ground, he should start to hiss, suddenly lunge at his enemy, throw up his head in mid-attack, stretch his wings and show off his magnificent chest, a great hero in dazzling white, at the sight of whom dogs cower, their tails between their legs, and horses stiffen their necks and shy sideways and quiver. But Glinski is standing on the threshhold, apparently quite calm, one eye half closed. Just

8

you come here, you black pip-squeak. Just fancy that, Feller, what will the creature do next? It acts one way and you know what to expect, but not every time. Of course, the world can be nicely arranged, in chapter and verse even, then everything fits together: geese behave in one way, horses in another, and then, all of a sudden, it won't fit together at all because a gander, by the name of Glinski either does not possess, or will not display, the manners befitting to a goose. He just stands there, this Glinski, blinks, and that's all.

Feller, who exorcises devils, but only from human beings, who dabbles his long fingers in the unholy turmoils of the souls entrusted to him, who, Sunday after Sunday, calls the preacher at Malken a deceiver and son of the devil, a Jerobeam or Rehabeam, in a loud voice which sends shivers up the spines of the women, young and old, but mostly the widows, Feller lets his arms drop, holds the books in front of him, suddenly shivery all over, gazes heavenwards and directs a troubled cry both to heaven and the house.

So he has looked up and called Christina, and Glinski must have noticed that the moment has passed, he has missed his golden opportunity for charging the black pip-squeak in the legs, that moment which makes life worthwhile and sheds glory on a hero for the rest of his days. Glinski has let it slip by. He stands there, blinks, looks placid, shuts one eye completely, bends his neck, peers in the hall and even steps aside. Now shoo, says Christina, occupying the doorway and slipping into the clogs which are waiting by the door, she comes towards Feller and says: Good Day, brother Feller, and Feller answers, mildly reproachful: God bless you.

Come in, says Christina and the old hero Glinski stares at Feller's black back disappearing into the house in front of Christina. He turns tail and marches off across the yard, the turkeys retreat too and the swallows put the finishing touches to their patterns in the sky. Christina emerges from the house with two baskets and runs to the shed. One basket of wood and one of peat.

Well, that's the second sentence. A little long, but it's not finished yet. Feller is indoors now, in the living-room, where my grandfather is sitting, but he still can't stop shivering; he has come on account of a baptism. And that's really the finest subject you can mention amongst Baptists, for it brings archangels and patriarchs winging to the room, their mouths agape, and the Gospel Songster and Voice of the Faith harmonise with bugle calls which make Glinski's trumpet seem piteous, a mere wailing flute.

My grandfather is sitting there muttering to himself as Feller enters, hands raised to heaven, and loudly utters the single word Johann. Stress on the second syllable, Johann!

Now what?

Listen to me before you speak, Feller implores, did you or did you not say: I and my house, we will serve the Lord? Last year at Whitsun? Did you say that?

What are you getting at, this isn't like you, answers my grandfather.

We sigh.

But not Alwin, his mouth is like a grinder's behind.

That's one of Grandma Wendehold's expressions. She's sitting by the stove in spite of the fact that it's summer, and Feller has paid no attention to her, she sits there like a picture from a stately home. The gently sloping vertical lines which guarantee the fine severity of such drawings are due to lack of teeth in her case and to the fact that her arms are hunched close together, the black stripe on her neck between the third and fourth chins takes the place of the velvet ribbon, only the medallion is missing.

She is sitting in the fireside chair, having drawn up the table, and is dealing cards, a grubby little pack which she carries around in her apron pocket, and, because she's always been one for tidiness of a quick and easy fashion, she takes the short cut with everything, and that includes cards. The king of hearts is always at hand; cards that have been thumbed as much as these match human lives, so tattered are they.

Olga, now you be quiet, says my grandfather.

At one time they had an affair, those two, well that's how rumour has it, long ago when my grandfather was a boy, which is easy to imagine, and when Olga Wendehold was a young girl—that's a little more difficult, but it's too long ago and she'll be ten years or so older than grandfather, and afterwards anything there was between them petered out because Grandma Wendehold joined the Adventists a long time ago, and my grandfather the Baptists, also long ago, and he even became an Elder of the church, and that too, a long time ago.

The fact that Grandmother Wendehold is nevertheless sitting here between the stove and the table with her cards in front of her, quite disposed to talk, is on account of the pigs. Because the old boy is afraid they'll contract red murrain and because a certain thick-leaved herb is extremely propitious for red murrain, but the most certain cure of all is Grandma Wendehold herself who understands all about the herb. Feller takes a seat.

In the church at Malken there is an altar which is perhaps not familiar to everyone. It's an ancient thing, carved out of wood, painted and fairly high up. The middle consists of nothing but waves, beautiful and blue as water should be, and sometimes is, although maybe not in the Drewenz or the Vistula, but certainly in the far-off Jordan, rows and rows of wavy lines, one behind the other. And on the right hand side stands John the Baptist, tall and haggard. The figure possesses neither stature nor beauty; it is stretching out an inconceivably thin arm, but thinner still are the hairy legs, which are planted in the water and disappear just above the knees into that famous camelhair robe.

I'm sure nobody knows quite how to carve camelhair out of wood. This is simply rough, with little points, nobbles, ridges and tuftlets, painted grey, and is meant to look untidy but imagine a workman's concept of disorder in wood carving, holy disorder at that. Not surprisingly it's a masterpiece of successful deliberation. Nevertheless John still looks fearsome enough. The wild honey which nourished him has certainly given him an aura more wild than sweet, particularly around the eyes, the very prominent nose and the chin. He's gazing forwards and sideways simultaneously, at the one he is to baptize, kneeling on the bank, which obviously necessitated a squint. Otherwise he's very lean and haggard, everyone knows that apart from wild honey, he survived on a diet of locusts. It's just as well the altar reminds us of one who had a harder life than a cottager in any Polish village who would have two pigs after all, and if not a cow, then at least three goats. Anyway that's all a thing of the past. And the Germans—Ragolski, Wistubba and Koschorrek, to name a few more, know that efficiency pays, whereas the Poles think everything comes from the Virgin Mary. But naturally she has more effect on the personality than the purse, so they say, and that's why the Poles have less, so they say.

Back to John the Baptist. He is on the altar at Malken, in the protestant church and the figure kneeling beside him is Jesus, it all took place on the Jordan long ago. Jesus on his bank is modest and fairly short and far less emaciated than the mighty locust-eater in the water. The artist has furnished the ground on which he is kneeling with an abundance of little round stones, he should try kneeling on it.

But that too has improved with time. Nowadays, when parents bring an infant to church for baptism they don't even see the lovely baptismal picture, they are far too occupied wearing down their bawling bundle with rocking and cooing and the wagging of fingers and rattles in an effort to induce sleep. The vicar doesn't see it either, because he's busy talking and everything here belongs to him anyway, however he still points to the scene once: that's the way it was in those days! Only the godparents look at it and are content with the way of the world, and the Baptists have seen it, of course. Jesus is certainly the least suspect of the witnesses, there's no question of referring to child-baptism, it shouldn't be called baptism at all when such a tiny infant is carted to the font, it doesn't even realise what's happening to it, poor thing. Baptism?

And that's why the reverend Feller insists on calling it 'sprinkling'. And again with emphasis: sprinkling. And my grandfather, who ought to be in agreement with him, my grandfather, as elder of the Baptist community of Neumühl, says: Now hold your peace, do.

Such strange behaviour. Now Feller must mount his high horse immediately and take up arms—he's fumbling about with his left foot in the stirrup but can't quite get hold of the reins, to grasp them he must put down the Voice of Faith and the Gospel Songster and just as he does that Grandma Wendehold launches a splendid flank attack from the stove.

Well Alwin, it does make me think.

What? asks Feller, unsuspectingly, but the crafty old woman has snared him now, and he hasn't even noticed.

Well Alwin, says Grandma Wendehold, it seems to me that that must be the reason the little children cry as much too, when they are baptized.

Well naturally, continues Feller, naturally, and then again, naturally. He certainly didn't expect help from this quarter, but somehow he's missed the line of battle, the horse has escaped him completely now, for Grandma Wendehold is laughing and my grandfather is laughing too, and he realises they are referring to the last ceremony in the Baptist community, when sister Marthe, a late candidate in her forties, screamed so loudly when the cold water hit her.

O dearest Feller, don't drown me! That sounded fine in chapel. And everyone stood around the baptistry, the elders at the front, the back rows hissing to Marthe to calm down and the others hissing at those at the back to be quiet, and my grandfather, right at the front, being an elder, saying: But Marthe dear, it's all right; now, now it's only the once.

What can Feller say now? Perhaps that the baptistry is to blame, and the fact that the community does not possess a contrivance like the chapel in Briesen: sunk in the floor, with steps leading down from both sides, quite convenient and supplied by the water main.

Just listen to that: water mains!

In America, informs Feller, every community has such things, but they get something together there, everyone gives his tithe over there, without a murmur, whereas you just murmur and give nothing. America, says Christina who has arrived with the jacket-potatoes, and my grandfather silently supplements: America my arse. Which is quite a customary sentiment. But he says nothing. Neither can Grandma Wendehold say anything at the moment, for one thing her card-game won't come out, the Jack of Clubs keeps turning up in the wrong place, and for another, anybody religious, who has any pride at all, has relatives in America and you never wish ill on relatives who are in the money, and anyone living so far away is always in the money—it's in every letter. Apparently a few have returned who really did own something out there—by way of that which a religious person would call the tangible blessings of God.

Christina has come in and put down the dish of potatoes. Next come plates and so forth, promptly as ever, and finally the bacon sauce.

Ugh! everything pickled again, grumbles Grandma Wendehold.

You don't have to eat it, retorts my grandfather. Johann, there's no need to go acting like a bear with a sore head again, returns Christina.

Perhaps the reverend Feller is thinking that it's now up to him to restore domestic harmony, but there's no need. Christina places the sauce on the table, grandfather pulls up his chair and in doing so farts. He derives no satisfaction from it, only a certain sense of shame: it could have been the scraping of a chair, or so he would like to think, but as no one is ever really taken in he says with deliberate heartiness: Well let's tuck in.

Olga Wendehold collects up her cards; it won't come out—all clubs and spades, no hearts at all, and heaves herself up from the chair by the stove. That's because the Adventists stand on account of it being written in Matthew 26 'sit down at table' and that's only possible if you have been standing or walking or some such thing just previously. Feller is still on his feet after his Crusade, which really left him flat on his backside, so he remains standing and folds his hands, still standing. Grandfather and Christina, having just sat down, are obliged to stand again: now they are all standing. Feller is reciting his long grace. Olga Wendehold's face is suitably demure, eyes closed, nose tilted downwards and lips as tight as a button-hole. Only when Feller says 'Enjoy and see how gracious is the Lord', does her breath quicken and her eyes open involuntarily, and then she sees before her the food she certainly won't enjoy; but she had already registered her disapproval, so she joins in softly, like the others, with Amen. Only Feller says it aloud. Now everyone may be seated again.

Ugh! potatoes in their jackets again, grumbles grandfather.

I'm peeling some for you now, soothes Christina.

God's good gift, says Feller grasping a potato and then recoiling immediately—it's still piping hot.

There you are, you should have been apprenticed with the smithy, scorns Grandma Wendehold. But let's get down to some plain speaking. Feller is content for the potatoes to be simply potatoes, and, after a crushing remark aimed at Grandma Wendehold—which is only natural as she's an outsider—an Adventist, he leans back in his chair, mindful of the purpose of his visit and says: In Malken your brother Gustav is having a baby sprinkled, by Glinski.

There it is, speaking plainly and now it's been said, we'll carry on with the conversation, though perhaps we'll speak less plainly—for we all know what plain speaking means and we'd rather keep the peace.

Perhaps you think it's none of my business, begins Alwin Feller, but it does concern me, especially with you as a church elder.

Don't make mountains out of molehills, retorts grandfather

You take it all too lightly, reproves Feller, last year, when you were with your brother in Malken you took communion from Glinski, don't contradict me, I know. There are brothers who do that sort of thing, but we do not. Open communion, as it's called, is not our wont and custom, nor will it be so in my lifetime.

You and your wont and custom. I think you'd do better to get on with your dinner.

No, Christina, says Feller, first of all Johann will say in front of both of us—he's now totally ignoring the existence of

16

Grandma Wendehold—he'll say whether or not he intends to go to Malken.

Well, brother Feller, now let me tell you something.

And grandfather does tell him something, all about peace and what that means, and the villager not envying the townsman, and the peacemakers being blessed. All excellent proverbs and quite becoming to an elder of the community, except that Feller has not come to bring peace, but a sword, and they are not getting very far; in the meantime, the food is still waiting, the potatoes are cold, there's a skin on the sauce and Christina is irritable, all because of this Feller. Now she joins in: If Gustav has his child baptized in Malken, that's his affair. Am I my brother's keeper? That's what it says in the Good Book.

Now that's all wrong. Cain's idle excuse is, at most, acceptable as an admission of guilt, certainly not as a defence. But this is where grandfather is in his element: Now you hold your tongue, Aunt Wife! And then to smooth everything over immediately: Has a woman ever been known to utter one sensible word? He remembers the sigh, which sounds quite authentic and even manages to rustle up his black look: the lower lids creep upwards, the eyes, which normally have something of the glazed stare of the habitual drinker about them, alter radically, the whites sparkle and the orbs darken, the little reddish veins disappear altogether and the normally brownish hued irises become quite black. There's nothing more that Feller can say now but: You think it over Johann.

What are you going to do with the old boy? How can you fight him, when he won't take up a stand? And this right here in your parish, Feller! Is he really going to Malken to take part in the whole heathen procedure, maybe even as godfather, what then? A church-elder. And it would be the one with the most money. Everyone who's anyone in the village listens to him. And if I take up a firm stand as the vicar, he'll answer: I'm coming to take communion, and he'll come, and I can't turn him away, that wouldn't do at all, I'll ruin my own congregation and he knows that as well as I do.

Feller, get up on your feet, you've lost the taste for food. Leave them to it and talk it over again with Barkowski and Rocholl, but what will be the use?

Feller, it's just not your day for winning battles. It started off all wrong with Glinski, that devil of a gander. If only I knew why the old boy wants to go to Malken; since when has he been so worried about his relatives, he's nothing to gain from them. There's something behind all this, I'm sure. He's a fine one to talk of peace! You're right there, Feller, there was something, in the spring, the whole village knows, but no one talks about it, except maybe the Poles—and they only whisper. You won't mention it either, Feller.

And now grandfather gets up, the silence has begun to weigh heavy at table, who knows where Feller's thoughts will wander if he's allowed to sit here much longer. I'm just going across to the mill, says grandfather, and you'd better be off home, Brother Feller, or mother will be cross.

His tone is jovial and Aunt Wife smiles, albeit a trifle acidly, she stands up and departs with Olga Wendehold, we must see to the pigs.

So Feller leaves, and grandfather goes to the mill. Half a mile away. He doesn't have to accompany Feller as the path to the mill leads away from the village straight past Pilch's cottage to a small tributary of the Drewenz. Well, good-bye then Alwin. God be with you, Johann.

Pilch's cottage. Four rooms. Thatched roof. The Pilchowskis used to live there. Pilchowski, who moved to Osterode and called himself Pilch, which is just as Polish but not so conspicuous. Sold up what he owned, all except for the cottage, no one wants to buy a shack like that. That's why, I suppose, it doesn't really belong to anyone, and that's why the gypsy Habedank lives there with his sister, or daughter or great aunt—you never know with gypsies—the girl Marie.

Grandfather is loitering there like a tramp. He peers around craning his neck. Nothing stirs. They're gadding about again, those gypsies. He goes up to the window, mutters something, shakes his fist, pauses a moment and turns round. Then back along the mill-path. Around the corner of the barn, and he comes into view. For the men sitting in front of the mill, that is.

Filthy pig, says Korrinth to Nieswandt, piddling up here again.

Let's get inside, says Nieswandt to Korrinth.

So he won't know they've sat around out here, he can't see this far, he'll only be able to deduce from the number of sacks that they just loaf around when he's not standing over them, but he knows that anyway. Old devil, says Korrinth to Nieswandt.

This is the way they talk about my grandfather. The Poles. It's not a straight path to the mill. It bends round and comes up from the South West, against the flow of the current, past the spot where they built the weir, the stakes are still there and the posts and boards and bundles of brushwood. Everything still lying around, fumes grandfather and now he has reached the mill. I told you to clear it all away. He's inside now. His voice is so loud that he leaves the door open. But Korrinth's voice is just as powerful, he shouts: No cart, just pick it up and carry it, is that the idea? And settles himself, legs wide apart, to search for snuff in his jacket-pockets, he manages to raise his left fist to the dilated nostril, thumb pointing upwards to form a hollow behind the joint for the

19

tobacco, but before the pinch of snuff can permeate his right
nostril, grandfather is off again: What do you mean pick
it up and carry it, wasn't there anyone here today?

What's the good of that, says Nieswandt, they load up and
clear off. Why should they bother themselves with this rubbish. And he adds, in a more friendly tone: Levin was here.
Korrinth has got the snuff to his nose, he sniffs a couple of
times and, in the interval before the sneeze overtakes him,
says: He sends his best wishes.

Grandfather controls his anger and subsides into his black
look: So Levin was here and everything's still lying around,
that suits him fine. But soon it won't matter anyway. It's
high time I went to Malken. And you can't rely on these
Polacks. Korrinth sneezes and grandfather warns: Don't let
that fellow set foot inside my mill, do you hear?

Didn't want to come in, says Nieswandt.

And now, in my grandfather's shoes, it would be nice to
know if that fellow, the Jew, said anything. And what he
wanted here anyway. But, in my grandfather's shoes, one
knows just what the answers will be: Didn't say anything,
just Good Day. On his way to see Marie.

Yes, we know all about Pilch's cottage. And this girl Marie,
that the fellow drags around with him. There's nothing more
to be gained here, so, black look, and away. Sacks counted,
instructions given for tomorrow.

If only I didn't have to see to every little thing myself. Look,
the paddle is hanging, no, not on the axle, down there on
the wheel, of course, look at it, damn it man! where else?
the paddles must be firm, if water gets inside, it just rushes
straight past if they're loose, can't you see that for yourself?
oh well, it's all the same to you anyway.

Sometimes, just as now on the way home, grandfather wishes
he had never got involved in the whole stinking mess—it's a

'stinking mess' already. But then: Oh well! Followed by the legitimate consideration: That's all I needed, that Jew setting himself up in business here. That's the way it is in the milling trade: whoever has to fetch the corn himself from the ends of the earth, soon winds up, but he didn't have to, they brought it to him, even the Neumühl farmers, I should have been on my guard then, Like Poleske.

Now, we come across a certain Poleske. Whom we haven't met before. Who is an ancestor, a sort of pet ancestor—we'll explain that later. Ah! says my grandfather, ah! he was a fine one and no mistake.

And now it's night-time. And grandfather is in bed. Christina is sleeping, but he is awake, and now he has a vision, if that's possible, so:

VISION NUMBER ONE

The republic of Poland was a kingdom which allowed every aristocrat to have his say. Ideally, and under the provisions of the constitution of Radom, they would all say the same, but that doesn't work. Earlier, in Poland, it would have been easier if everyone had said something different. But as every Pole is an aristocrat, and every single one is related to one of the royal families, and every ordinary family is older than royalty anyway, everyone is of equal birth rank. Thus the Poles are all blue-blooded, and the Germans, who were Polish but have now been or considered themselves to be German for as many generations as they can muster, are, if possible, even more so.

Well that's one version of the history of the Polish republic, which can be heard, if only you have the patience to listen and can find the right sort of authority on the subject. One like my grandfather for instance. Who rambles on and on, over one glass, a second, third and fourth: all about the old days.

The vision belongs to medieval history, where we encounter the nobility which is so proud of holding itself in such high, self-endowed esteem, and, as everyone is an aristocrat anyway, the entire noble nation is familiar with it, including the descendants, smallholders, relatives, in-laws, homes for widows, young ladies' seminaries in Cracow, commissariats for entail, children's skittles, foundlings and Germans. A thorough knowledge of history is a universal characteristic, one is at home with one's ancestors and expects visions, it's quite normal and nothing like as sensational as in Berlin or Mecklenburg-Strelitz, when the pallid wife of the Hohenzoller appears to him clad in silk or fustian, according to the season, or when the chief ancestor of some Junker appears to him clad in leather or chains according to the curse of some village maid or shepherd. You just expect visions and think nothing of them, everyone has them, including my grandfather, of course.

Grandfather is lying in bed, brooding and muttering as the vision enters, it has a short black beard, and the name of Poleske, and is an ancestor, and is standing in the bedroom saying something. And grandfather replies, and then Poleske, always the same words, time after time, like magic incantation, but simple: My Right. In capital letters. It's clear the world cannot be in agreement with it. My grandfather has His Right, but it must be respected by everyone, otherwise it would not be a Right and would be of no use to him, so: My Right. And then Poleske vanishes again, between the shutters or out of the door.

Poleske made up his mind to do something and acted accordingly. He stood up for something he believed in. And this story of his ancestor has a very sweet taste for my grand-

22

father, a sweetness which is connected with His Own Right.

But first, Poleske's story. Briefly, it goes like this: Poleske is lying strapped to the block, face downwards. The henchman raises his sword to shoulder-level and drops it swiftly, severing head from body. The judges linger a moment, it's all over rather quickly and it was in a public square too, but there were no people, no spectators. This sort of thing is depressing without spectators. Just women and children. Then, briskly, everything is packed away, sawdust and sand are strewn on the ground. The women take their children home. The priest attaches himself to them. He knows all about it, Mattern convicted himself, he says, under torture.

The weather is fine with scarcely any sea breeze, the town's spires glow red against the watery blue sky. God had mercy on Poleske, with all that lovely sunshine, the mothers tell their children.

The crow, strutting diagonally across the path with deliberate, heavy tread, suddenly trips a couple of steps, falters, stretches its wings, hops sideways, waits a moment and then, calmly as before, goes on its way past the ash tree towards the field.

Mattern, who is standing in the middle of the path with some of his followers, his hand on Poleske's saddle, says placidly: The old bird just felt like dancing, it doesn't mean a thing, but Poleske growls down from the saddle: Let her dance, you're some robber! and: There she goes.

That crow is no hawk he thinks, and the day's not done till the hawk cries, for that we must wait.

They have come rather far into Danzig territory. But they are in a position that is too good to lose, so the spies have been keeping watch for a couple of hours now, in the wood to the north. My hawks, muses Poleske, who cry so well, short and sharp, so that only we hear it. And then it means: sideways.

I'll be over there, says Mattern, and he turns and trudges down the path. His men follow, one after the other. It's the same every time, the waiting, the grouping, the positioning of Mattern's band: behind the bushes. The horses some distance away, in the fir copse. When the Danzigers approach, go down to the road and hold them up—the usual forty coaches, and then the hawks cry and Poleske's men come over the field from the wood, and Poleske himself rides up slowly. Your money or your life, always the same. With seventeen arquebuses. We never lived like this on the Oder, the old fellow pays, and then there's half the booty. It'll be warm enough for us in Poland this winter, Mattern reflects, and it's autumn already.

Poleske and his horse, alone on the road. Night is falling. They won't come now. As though they can smell danger. Yet we've never waited here before. Mattern advised against it: too near the Vistula, you are only open on one flank. Yet it's really two. He knows quite a bit. He's always wanting to go back west. That's where he's from.

Poleske, the hawk, tugs the reins a little and rides up the path to the wood.

Old Gregor hobbles up to him. Nothing, master. Send me Martin, says Poleske. Someone must tell Scholz at Dirschau. The others can go home. Take Mattern's men with you.

It's dark, like Poleske's empty house. To which he won't return till he has changed the minds of the Danzigers about invading the republic with their covered waggons. Our lands are being eaten away. Those hagglers from Thorn and Cracow are wheedling their way in, and the king sees it all and holds up his hand, he needs something for his trade with princesses, here a little light and here a little shade on the paths of deceit.

And so the crown of Poland teeters: a paunch and port-face, *pacta conventa* and *vota* of every kind hung round a bull-neck. He, Poleske, has a task to accomplish here.

Certainly to defend the honour of the Republic, and the Right, Poland's Right, honour and Right which can be helped with excursions, insurrections, stock-taking decisions, protests and finally, great displays of piety in Gnesen or Tschenstochau. But perhaps more profitably here, where Poleske is cleaning up the scum which has spread itself around the creek and is menacing the republic. That's why he fetched Mattern's crowd from the Oder, that's why he dropped everything; one fine day, leaving the women to muddle along in the meantime as best they could, that's why they are lying around here in the sand, and behind the bushes, four hundred men. And they know him now, the gentlemen from Danzig, and stay at home.

I'll be off to Wirschau, says Martin.

You go to Scholz. He'll tell you everything. And to the priest at Schönsee. I want to know whom the king's judge, Pampowski, has ordered to Marienwerder.

Martin is back the following evening. The Danzigers won't come again. They've set 600 Guilders on his, Poleske's head, and as many on Mattern's black head and issued a free pardon.

So I can sell Poleske for 600 Guilders, grins Mattern.

Alive, says Poleske and rides away.

Pampowski has summoned every creature available with no success, just another little manœuvre of episcopalian sees, profitable to both the Danzigers and His Majesty, and Weisselrode still retains the crook in his gouty fingers.

Half a day's ride from Marienwerder Poleske is taken prisoner. He is alone. Pritschmeister takes him into custody in Danzig. He was waiting.

The trial is brief. Citizen Scholz or the priest at Schönsee, Poleske wonders. Two days later the warder tells him through the door that Mattern is in the next cell. How long has he been there. Poleske asks, but no answer. Or Mattern, he wonders. The following noon he is led out to the square. No chains. The town guards at a distance.

Poleske walks slowly. But the town, this arid cluster of stones, seems to fly past his eyes. It is as if everything were bathed in moonlight, no shadows. Only, now, in the air, a shriek. Poleske looks up in the watery sky, shades his eyes with his hand and looks again. A hawk is pursuing a lark. He dives down on it. Reprieve. The lark soars above him. Not for a second does she cease her tremulous song.

The column has halted. Now it moves off again. The sheriff takes up his position. There is the place of execution. He will stand here, he, Poleske, who had a duty to fulfil, who was in luck for a couple of months and then his luck deserted him.

He stands in the middle of the huge square. It is noon. The 28th September, 1516. A brilliant autumn. Poleske takes a couple of steps forward. Again the cry of the hawk. But no one looks up. And now, all is quiet.

You can hear the silence.

And now one ought to speak of the moon, of the water, where the mill stands, where the weir used to be, one mill, but no longer the other.

Christina pants a little in her sleep.

Ah! Well, says my grandfather, and perhaps he's thinking: Those were the days, and now a Jew tries to kick me in the pants, to think it could come to that, but I'll go to Malken, they'll all hold their tongues, I'll turf those Polacks out of the mill, they can clear off, into the Russian territory, it'll cost money but then that Levin can talk as much as he likes.

Go crawling to the court at Briesen, you skinny Jew. They'll piss all over you, we're Germans here, in case you hadn't realised. At any rate he, my grandfather, is already quite sure, who will do the pissing, and with whom. My Right, he says.

CHAPTER TWO

It is a good three hours' drive by cart to Malken. And as Malken lies quite a way to the north of the Drewenz and all the tributaries and mill streams remain in the Drewenz valley, though the land is quite flat, the Chaussee never touches water, not even the tiniest stream; who ever has to water his horses, does so in Gronowo at the pump in front of the tavern or in Trzianek, or he makes adequate provision beforehand to cover the twenty four kilometres, even in July. The road is called the Chaussee and we'll keep that name.

Starting in the middle of the village is a cobbled pavement which lasts for a good half kilometre, the left side is not paved at all and it's only a summer road, then the cobbled path gives way to a simple sandtrack, in the village of Gronowo a sort of rough gravel path has been stamped out, and then, because of the different soil, there is a slippery clay path and shortly before Trzianek the cobbles start up again; so it goes on, as soon as you are used to one sort of surface, you meet another, and, even if you encounter the same sort of paving, or lack of it, twice, each surface is always worse than the previous one, all of which offers an adequate explanation of my grandfather's increasingly surly temper.

Grandfather is on his way to Malken. With a horse-drawn cart. He is in a bad mood, and is sitting there to the right of Aunt Wife, holding forth about the locality, the economics of property, and the price of an acre of field or pasture, and who would sell and who would not. In spite of the fact that Christina knows considerably more about it as they approach

Malken, as she is from here, to be exact: from Brudzaw, from Little Brudzaw. So: Brunowski's father-in-law did a deal with Konarski in Dombrowken, way back in '62, for 70 Talers—but who is interested in all that? Christina sits next to grandfather, she is wearing her hat for the first time this year. Let's hear something about Christina. Christina, *née* Fagin, addressed in the community as Sister or Christina and by my grandfather as Aunt Wife, is exactly twenty years younger than grandfather, his second wife, with no children, endowed by grandfather with 7,000 Talers, which are still untouched, in the bank at Kowalewo-Schönsee, to which the children from the first marriage, the stepsons and stepdaughter, are not entitled, although they consider themselves to be—they could point out that Christina would have no objection, just the two old men, Fagin in Little Brudzaw and my grandfather. Nevertheless the stepsons call her Aunt, and the stepdaughter Christina, and my grandfather says Aunt Wife which is meant to sound conciliatory to the family, and does not. More about Christina.

She's a pretty woman. A little plump, a little shorter than usual for the Fagin family, but still half a head taller than my grandfather, which is held against her in the community, not so much the actual height though, which is the will of God, but rather the fact that Christina makes no attempt to compensate for her size, which was obviously inflicted upon her as a temptation or spiritual trial, by adopting a suitably humble stance and manner of speech, in other words the fact that she has omitted to correct that with which God has endowed her, which one would assume to be an act of pride rather than humility if one does attempt it—anyway Christina makes no effort to do so, and, in the eyes of every righteous soul, in Neumühl at any rate, this very omission is designated as pride. And held against the person in question. More about Christina. She is loud and cheerful and sings: 'Heart, my heart, say, when will you be free' . . . a favourite melody such as you might hear in the kitchen, woodshed or cellar, even if maybe not in chapel on Sunday with a nice vocal arrangement, with pauses for the soprano, short solo spots for the bass, while alto and tenor are not quite sure where to join in and waver uncertainly, which is in itself quite effective—even if it isn't sung in chapel on Sunday, from the Voice of Faith or the Gospel Songster, but mostly from memory, it could be considered unsuitable, by righteous souls that is, for what does she mean by free? She can't be feeling well; Isn't it absolute heaven with Johann? The children gone and still so much money there! Particularly now that Levin has tippled off with his mill!

But no, they don't all think like that, not even all the congregation. It was so convenient with Levin, they think, he bought and paid cash, now you can cart the corn all over the countryside if you only want to sell it and not have it ground. In this new Empire you need money, in other words you have to pay for everything, with Groschen and Taler, and as many of them as possible. The only trouble was, you couldn't let the old boy know that you were selling to Levin, that would rile him, it's only natural.

Now that's been stopped, and quite a blow it was, but no one complains, they simply say: Well Johann, you showed him where to get off all right, he won't come again. And: Thank God! But what of Christina?

As we said, Christina is from Brudzaw, Little Brudzaw, which lies behind Malken, in the direction of Strasburg. It's quite pretty there. Here the chain of mountains stretching across from the northern sweep of the Drewenz falls away in the meadows with two or three last spurs, and to the west, where it is completely flat, the good soil starts for corn and sugar beet, there is a round lake, and behind that extensive pine forests, yes it's very pretty, Christina comes from there, and it all matches her.

Now they are three kilometres outside Malken. And it's nearly six o'clock. They set off at three. There was no sign of Feller.

Mind you, grandfather didn't risk driving through the village, but took the horses round the barn and along the path to the Chaussee, as yet not at all pretentious, but then, on the Chaussee, just before Gronowo, he lays aside the whip and lights a cigar and feels like a judge, or the Polish count in Ciborz, or as if he had just shit in the Black Sea.

So they have come through Gronowo and Trzianek too. In Trzianek grandfather had to stop twice for Christina to speak to Rocholl's aunt and another old woman—it is so easy to confuse them, they all look alike, and now they are three kilometres from Malken. Trzianek saw the last of the trees lining the Chaussee, now, above the horses' heads you can trace the plains stretching into the distance.

The road leads straight to the village, which for the time being, occupies the space between the left ear of the left horse and the right ear of the right horse. To the left of the right ear of the brown, that is the left horse, the church spire emerges and now, exactly mid-way between the ears of the pie-bald, that is the right horse, you can pick out the village tavern, and next to that, more towards the left ear, the tiled roof of the school, and in between the two is Gustav's house, and then there is something that you don't see if you look through grandfather's eyes, clusters of chestnut and lime trees, hedges and orchards, lilac and elder bushes. But now it's becoming impossible to accommodate and divide it all between the horses' ears, the village is after all, getting nearer, two storks are visible circling over the roof of the church, and now the horses won't hold their ears still enough, they must be able to hear something, and that too is a sign that it's not far now to Malken. But as we have been concerning ourselves with Christina, Christina, *née* Fagin, worth 7,000 Talers, Sister and Aunt Wife, we will occupy the rest of the journey with a short description of grandfather, and why only short description? We are still a good two kilometres from Malken. They say that in his youth, my grandfather was a narrow-chested, somewhat unprepossessing individual, so they say, 1 metre 66 in stockinged feet, but he must have become taller with the advancing years. I wouldn't know whether or not he has grown physically, it must be the dignity and general affluence, but now he is most imposing, particularly on a Sunday when his gold watch-chain hangs across his paunch, indeed he is at his most magnificent, when he's drunk, then, on the left as you face him, his liver swells impressively. A man and a German and my grandfather.

He is sitting on his carriage, up on top, he throws away a cigar stub, the third today, and takes up the whip again. He is thinking. And what's in his mind! First take Gustav aside, that had better be this evening, then tomorrow Glinski, just pass the time of day first, then see to the rest in the afternoon between coffee and a couple of brandies, it will have to sound good, maybe it will need money, we shall see.

We know something about the locality now: the corner between Thorn, Briesen and Strasburg, where the Drewenz, coming down from the Löbau district to the north-east, flows into the Vistula south of Thorn just after Leibitsch, after forming the boundary with Russian Poland or 'Kongress-Poland' from Cielenta, opposite Strasburg, the Culmerland, an ancient and pious district, where the rich in money or honour are German and proud of their noble heritage, which is Polish, but that was a long time ago, and now, to be precise in 1874, one is, in the person of my grandfather, pious—that is a

Baptist—and nevertheless on the way—with a horse drawn cart—to the enemies of the Faith—that is the Protestants—about to defend one's Rights—as a German—and all this because one is the owner of a mill near Neumühl, on one of the right hand tributaries of the Drewenz, which never leaves Polish territory although it is sandwiched between Germany and Russia, a water mill, with a mill pond and, if one so desires, a weir too.

The rubbish is still lying about on the bank: stakes, posts, boards, planks and bundles of brushwood—messy and ruined, and this mess of ruins belongs to our story, which has been our aim in view through all this chatter about my grandfather.

Levin is lying on the grassy slope, lying there on his back, his arms behind his head, long and skinny. He says: You mustn't keep on about it. And this Marie, whom Levin calls Marje, says: Yes, all right. I had a letter from my aunt, says Levin, I'm to go to Briesen, withdraw it all and come to Rozan, my people are there, and Marie is lying beside him in the grass and says: Yes, all right. And that is about the third sentence in our story.

If the two of them were to sit up, they would see at the foot of the slope the gangplanks, half submerged, and the firm patch of sand to which the steps lead down, fastened and reinforced with stakes and boards, the patch where Levin's mill used to stand, but they don't need to sit up, they know it all, that's where it stood, for a whole year and it was swept away with the weir water from the other mill, it broke up and was carried into the Drewenz, in the spring, when the water was cold, past a couple of villages, drift-wood, nothing more.

Only the mill-stones remained. They glisten there rearing up out of the rushing water which swills sand against them forming mounds, from the tip of which the grains fly over the mill-stones as if playing leap-frog.

All right, says Marie, and now this June is getting dark, the moon is over Russian-Poland, and why should it come over the river? Marie sees it, and Levin too, and she says: Better to stay.

Well then: you, moon, stay over Russian-Poland and you, Levin, stay here and don't go to your people in Rozan.

In a fortnight the trial opens.

CHAPTER THREE

Getting dark, says Habedank.

Sitting in front of Palm's tavern on the wooden steps like a gypsy, unsupported, one hand up on the railings, the other on the black violin-case, which resembles a Vistula-boat, sturdy and long and black, as we said, with a lid like the roof of a house.

And what does this Habedank fellow want in Malken? He came through here last week, from Cielenta, some horse-deal without money, sense or gypsy's oath, which is: right hand upwards, the other arm pointing down, but behind the back. And he passed Gustav—grandfather's heathen brother, as we recall—and Gustav gave him instructions for the music, for Sunday, when the baptism is over, for the affair afterwards, towards evening. You'll have music says Habedank as he departs.

And now he has returned, early on Sunday, with his violin, just as he usually comes to these affairs, because he is the music, the worldly music, happy or sad, one or the other, with nothing in-between and no transition: happy or sad. Just like Habedank's way of talking: either Rubbish or Very Nice. At the sight of the child he says, quite confidently: Nice little fellow.

Just a little further on is Gustav's house, between the church and the tavern, today the infant is being baptised, the seventh, straggler or barrel-scrapings, which is it?—christened with Protestants, by Glinski, who shouts so loudly, this infant which is so convenient for my grandfather, with its protestant baptism and so inconvenient for the reverend Feller with its heathen sprinkling.

The other children, Gustav's other children, all six of them, are playing in the garden, audibly. Habedank, the music man, can even make out six voices. They are singing:

> Squeak, shriek,
> Goose's beak,
> Goose's feet,
> Taste sweet.

It's a funeral song. The necessary dead swallow can always be found and it is buried with pomp, circumstance and song. At least this way the children aren't always under your feet. As Gustav's wife is just saying in the kitchen, saying to Christina that is, as she hovers over the eight pots on the stove and Christina hears the pretty song, which she knows, of course, and thinks back to their arrival yesterday evening. Grandfather and Christina came into the living-room, and the oldest two of Gustav's six, Christian and Emilie, were standing there to shake hands, but the other four were hiding under the big red sofa, four pairs of eyes, that's all you could see.

Till Christina delved down in her purse for the bag of aniseed balls. Then they emerged and stood for a moment, all six in a row, Christian at the front, then Emilie, according to size, with eighteen month intervals, now pounce on the bag, a handful for each in the little cupped fists, then retreat, four under the sofa, the older ones outside. There they sat, the little ones in safety with their sweets. Just like puppies said grandfather standing and gazing in mild astonishment, till Gustav remembered the three-year-old he particularly wanted him to see. So the men went out to the stables.

As it began to get dark, yesterday, when the children had

been fetched indoors or out from under the sofa to be put to bed, the first hurdle had already been crossed.

Gustav had warned the vicar's wife over the fence, and then my grandfather had knocked at the study door, and half an hour later Glinski had personally accompanied him to the gate and bidden him good-bye and: Till tomorrow then, and it is safe to assume that all has gone well so far from the way in which grandfather is now buttoning up his white shirt at half-past seven in the morning and simply tears out the hair which was daring to poke through his buttonhole, no time for trivialities. Aunt Wife, he says, where are my socks?

The socks are there, breakfast is there, everything is there, the infant swathed and adorned, Trude, the sister-in-law has taken charge of the pots. Christina and Gustav's wife are sheathed in tight black dresses. Everything ready. And Habedank is still sitting on Palm's steps.

Now the bell starts up and sounds like a tin bucket, and from behind Wyderski's barn Willuhn appears and catches sight of Habedank.

Has Palm shut up shop? Willuhn bawls, staggering across the street. When I was still at school, ho ho.

Willuhn is drunk again.

Habedank puts his violin one step higher behind him.

Willuhn, it should be noted, was once a teacher here in Malken. And could still be. But for the fact that a teacher simply must not get so drunk, at least not all the time. Why then? Willuhn married money, all went well for ten years, then they took his school away, no more money, Willuhn became a nuisance, so he crawled in with an old pensioned-off landowner, at the mine-work, also penniless, there they remain, eternally drunk, no one knows how they manage it. Willuhn is also a musician but there aren't that many functions and he can't play for long before getting drunk and all manner of things can slip out then. We can wonder at the whys and the wherefores, but Willuhn at any rate has already had his fill this morning, now he is standing by Habedank, he bows dangerously low and says much too loudly: Christina's old man is here. Arrived yesterday evening.

Yes, says Habedank, there he is.

My grandfather. Going to church. And Christina too, and Gustav, and Gustav's wife and old Fagin and Gustav's wife suddenly turns and bolts back into the house, not realising her unseemly haste till just in front of the door, she stops and walks in slowly, and shortly afterwards comes out of the door even more slowly and sees: there they all are, standing, waiting, and slowly she walks up to the group, which moves off again in silence.

She's just like a suet-pudding, says Willuhn. What, says Habedank, you can't have a black suet-pudding. Where's your instrument.

Hakedank says instrument, Willuhn says squeeze-box, it is an old fashioned concertina, held together with countless patches and pieces of cobbler's thread; it's not exactly ideal, and is rather prone to coming apart, and then emitting soft overtones, which come as an unpleasant surprise as they seldom harmonise with the melody in progress.

I've left it at Gustav's place, says Willuhn and sinks down on to the steps.

And on the other side of the street my grandfather has already observed: there's Habedank, what can that gyppo want?

He's coming to play tonight, Gustav explains, I told him to, why do you ask.

Oh, no reason, it's all right by me, says grandfather, but he is not at all happy, my grandfather, but now they have reached the church door, and here come the others, the Willutzkis, the Witzkes, the teacher's wife, the Jendreizycks, the Palms and goodness knows who else, now say Good Day, chat a little, everything fine, put on a good face, in to the church before the bellringing stops.

Now they are inside, says Habedank.

What can the old man want in Malken? Habedank has his own ideas. Does Willuhn know? But how could he?

But Willuhn does know.

Yesterday he was with Glinski, says Willuhn, yesterday evening, that Baptist with Glinski. There'll be a fine to do back at Neumühl.

There already has been, says Habedank, there already has been.

Feller is running around with a bee in his bonnet.

So how much does Willuhn know?

The old man has already seen the parson yesterday evening, and today he is going to his church, he's not letting Glinski slip through his fingers, he must have a reason.

Is it safe to question Willuhn? without him trumpeting around everywhere: Habedank did this and Habedank said that. But if he does know something, I reckon he'll talk.

One cautious question: What do you think, Willuhn, perhaps they were planning some business-deal with horses?

Fiddlesticks horses! you're always on about horses, says Willuhn.

It's his brother. He'll be godfather.

So Willuhn doesn't know anything? Habedank takes his violin, pulls himself up by the railings and goes.

Wait a minute, Willuhn calls, why are you running off?

But Habedank is in a hurry. This evening at Gustav's. I'll be there at five.

After a couple of strides Willuhn stops—Habedank really is running—and yells: Clear off then, Gypsy. Off to scratch a nag's arse again, with that violin of yours?

Stop here Willuhn, it's nothing to do with you, let Habedank run, it's not your worry, and if it were, it would only last until the next bottle. You don't know your way around all the confusion, that is known as Life or Piousness or Right, you finished with that, seven years' ago, when you got shot of the school, don't start it all over again, you're in a state of Innocence, possibly the only one in Malken who is, possibly the only one from here to Briesen, you don't ask where the next Schnapps will come from, it'll turn up somehow, consider the lilies of the field and the birds of the air. Go Willuhn, don't hang about. We'll meet again this evening at Gustav's. So, now the street is empty.

Only the storks are flying around. They suffered the same fate as Willuhn. Yesterday Gonserowski the verger, that ageing manikin, prized their nest off the church roof with a long pole. And that's unlucky too.

Habedank could tell you tales of the storks, they all come from Osienczna, which means stork's nest, in the Posen district, that's where they're from, and, as everyone knows, cartwheels are put on the roofs to encourage them to come and to make it comfortable for them, so that they stay and return next year. That's what they do. It's a new fashion not to allow them on the church roof, quite a new fashion.

Beneath, in the church, under the roof which is now empty, but encircled by two storks, they have reached the sermon hymn. Glinski stamps up the pulpit steps, acknowledges my grandfather with a friendly nod, then casts his eye over his flock. And we'll leave him to talk, or even shriek, it doesn't matter to us, provided that he doesn't forget the announcement of Gustav's seventh who is to receive Holy Baptism today, otherwise he can shout as much as he likes. And when church is over, they return, this time Gustav and his wife lead the way, my grandfather and Christina and old Fagin from Little Brudzaw following up, rather quicker than before. And then back in the church, this time with the infant, we are familiar with the rest. John the Baptist presiding from above, in his wooden Jordan, wooden legs and wooden camel-hair, all in life-like colours of course. Up aloft John baptises, down below Glinski baptises.

Not as nicely as the Baptists, is Christina's opinion, not so much ceremony. Grandfather is standing holding the baby on a cushion and after a while he hands it to Fagin, the other godfather. Gently, gently. The child receives a name and knows nothing about it, muses grandfather. Still, never mind, he says, so loudly that Glinski looks up, breaking off in the middle of his sentence.

He knows what comes next. Grandfather remains quite calm and says: Do continue, Reverend, and Glinski merely raises his eyebrows, albeit quite high and with a distinct jerk, before continuing, but grandfather is thinking: Don't make such a fuss, I treat my parson just the same.

We know all about that.

So the child receives its name, Christoph after Godfather Fagin and Johann after my grandfather. And it wasn't quite without ceremony, Christina at any rate is crying and Gustav's wife cannot sit and watch, she cries too, it lasts till they reach home, it does you such a power of good.

Palm's tavern will stay shut today, not only the front entrance which is always closed on a Sunday, but the back door too, the Palm's have been invited to the baptism, so it's no use Willuhn coming and knocking on the kitchen door for his quarter of spirits. He is standing there and shaking his head, poor Willuhn. My Life! There's never been anything like it, he mutters, utterly dejected, and spins round so quickly that he stumbles and falls flat on his face.

Any witness is swift to indulge in joyful indignation: Willuhn again, no, and on a Sunday too, drunk as a lord.

Whereas it was really only disappointment. We are all very quick to wrong a person, particularly when that person is Willuhn. Who is now slowly himself upright, first on one knee, then standing, then, without further ado he strides off, round Palm's house, through the entrance, along the right hand hedge towards Gustav's house.

He waits at the door. Goes in. Sets foot in the hall and suddenly halts in astonishment for Katy, Gustav's youngest, is standing in the doorway screaming at the sight of him. Which is really quite unfair of her as Willuhn has put on his Sunday best, he has come in socks and a hat, and his black bow is tied at the front, what's the matter with the child!

Come now, it's only Herr Willuhn, says Gustav's wife, Herr Willuhn, I expect you'd like a cup of coffee, wouldn't you, Herr Willuhn?

Yes, of course, a cup of coffee, Herr Willuhn answers sullenly, just what I wanted.

And here is the baptismal party.

Just as in the old days, Willuhn goes up to Glinski's wife, no thought of falling flat on his face now, Willuhn, teacher, retired.

Educated type, says Glinski amicably, that's quite obvious.

We'll let Glinski talk. Our story is beginning to take shape. We are approaching the fourth sentence. In a roundabout way.

And we are in the front parlour.

The long table has been pulled up in front of the new sofa with the brown supports. Old Fagin, my grandfather's father-in-law, is in the place of honour, next to him sits Christina, as his daughter, on the other side old man Palm, his elbows on the table, Parobbek that was, next to him in the velvet

chair Frau Palm, with the long neck and dark curly hair
reaching down to her shoulders, renowned for their beauty,
my grandfather always refers to her 'skinny frame', whom
Palm brought over from the Polish region—a pure German
family though, Hecht or some such name, then Gustav's
sister-in-law, and opposite her Tethmeyer, and at the top of
the table the Glinskis, in two armchairs, and my grandfather,
in the third armchair.

Must we describe it all?

A front parlour like so many other front parlours, and a
baptism-party is in progress, not too much fuss though, as we
see, a straggler is always rather embarrassing. When the infant
was on show earlier and the women were chattering and finding resemblances, above all with my grandfather, and Gustav
was putting on airs, Tethmeyer slapped the happy father on
the back and pointed out: You could have spared yourself
that one.

No, why should he.

They are still all seated round the long table. They have still
a long way to go with the food, the white cream cakes and
the dark fruit cakes.

And the children are not under the sofa. They are wandering
round the table, keeping an eye on what is eaten and what
is left, and singing of course, you can hear them, but not
distinctly, but maybe it's only lack of attention, as little Louis'
voice is quite audible singing: There won't be enough for
us, there won't be enough for us.

Gustav's wife is wielding the coffee-pot in the kitchen, grandfather and Christina are joining her in another cup, all good
things go in sevens, and Frau Glinski too, for company.

Willuhn, sandwiched between grandfather and the sister-in-
law, sips at his coffee but the rest will get cold, as opposite
him is Tethmeyer, the great joker. He can start a conversation

with Tethmeyer in the way that you always start one with him, as if you had to complete a sentence, the sentence you didn't finish yesterday or the day before, about the storks or sundry illnesses—Tethmeyer's particular interest. You can say: She'll not get well again, and Tethmeyer knows straightway that you mean Urbanski's grandmother, he just knows, he sits there like a huge owl, just about to spread its wings, as if peering inwards, at something which is not there yet, but which will arrive any minute. Eduard Tethmeyer, the undertaker, the huge owl, with upturned bushy brows over the half-closed eyes, which are as round as saucers when he does open them, with close-cropped grey skull and hairy ear-tips the huge owl, Eduard. He flits in and out of houses, bringing words of comfort to the sick-beds: You're looking fine again, it'll be all right, you can stake your life on it. And in the meanwhile the man Tethmeyer has sized up the patient and his parting words are: one metre, eighty.

So Tethmeyer is there, the owl of ill omen and the great joker. Opposite Willuhn, and on his left Gustav's sister-in-law, then the Palms.

There's never been anything like it! Sitting around here, the Palms, both of them, and the likes of us are run off our feet! But Willuhn, you don't say that kind of thing in front of a vicar, the Sabbath is holy, this time at the kitchen door as well, so let's get back to the table: Well, Eduard, how's business? That's hardly suitable either. Try again: Was it nice in the church? Did he bawl? Meaning the infant, not Glinski.

But Tethmeyer can safely ask: Who do you mean? As Glinski is not listening, but talking to my grandfather. You know, he says, as long as it's not in my village, I have no objection, and the Superintendent is totally in agreement with me. Decent folk, the Baptists, you only have to look at yourself.

But this is a disappointment for my grandfather, it's not leading anywhere, they'll never get down to business this way. Grandfather says: Quite so, Reverend, naturally, one is a man and has one's religion, just that everyone should mind his own affairs—perhaps grandfather has a point there. If you think about it: here in Malken you have the Protestants, they don't know each other, in Neumühl the Baptists all know each other, and at the Neumühl mine the Adventists do as well, there are two sides to everything, in Trzianek there are the Sabbatarians, in Kowalewo and Rogowo the Methodists, towards Rosenberg the Memmonite villages start, but that's further away.

Yes but, says Grandfather, and is, it seems to me, prepared, if need be, to sell out the Baptists to Glinski, out of a sense of Righteousness, as we well know. He may be, but the parson's lady wife is not, she is quite against it.

So she interrupts, she is namely from a good family and has a high-pitched voice, she takes one more gulp of coffee, crashes the cup down on the table, grasps her chignon as the new false plait won't stay on properly but drives out the hairpins and exclaims: no, my dear miller, that would only stir up discontent, you surely don't want that!

Our beloved imperial house, says Palm, who was in a cholera hospital during the war in 1870 for two weeks, carrying buckets. Yes, says grandfather, our beloved imperial house for ever. Yes, says Glinski, our beloved imperial house. Our imperial hero has just indicated by the repatriation law and the laws of the ninth of March—Yes indeed, affirms Frau Glinski, her noticeably straight nose in the air, fingering the little gold watch hanging round her neck on a long chain, he is perpetrating the work of our Doctor Martin Luther quite admirably.

There you are, you see, says grandfather.

But gentlemen, Glinski interpolates, that is intended against the enemy, the Romish church, and that means—

Against the Polacks, says grandfather.

If that's what you have in mind, says Glinski, you're quite right. Encircled as we are by a people fundamentally foreign to us—

Oh ho, thinks grandfather, now we've got him on the right tack. At the bottom of the table Willuhn gets flushed about the ears and says to Tethmeyer: Now he's in full swing, and leans back and folds his hands together, and Tethmeyer screws up the corner of his mouth to whisper: Hallelujah, then relaxes and says: We're off. Now one of Glinski's German Speeches.

Were the door not just opening at this very moment to reveal Habedank, black cap in hand, black violin case under his arm, then we would have to endure *Gloria et Victoria*. Well Habedank, you're more than welcome, you shall have coffee. Habedank says: Good evening all.

Gustav's wife says: Good evening, Herr Habedank.

Tethmeyer swivels round and calls out: Got your box ready?

Willuhn says: Five already?

And grandfather muses: Well he's steamed up all right, our man of God, we'll take him aside, over there by the round table, a cigar, a couple of brandies. What were you saying, Reverend? Oh yes, says Glinski, of course, we had a little chat yesterday. Natalie we have some business to attend to. But perhaps you would care to join us?

So Natalie joins them. Christina goes out into the kitchen to fetch glasses. Just as well, grandfather thinks, she's more than likely to come out with something quite unsuitable from the Bible.

One universal, holy, Christian Church. With this Frau Glinski harks back to the earlier conversation, and then she says: Pigs! referring to the Catholics, who are deplorable and Polish.

Glinski grasps a cigar and my grandfather hurriedly follows his example, he too, takes a cigar, bites off the point, puts the coloured paper-ring which Glinski has naturally left on his cigar, over the little finger of his left hand, in the meantime Natalie prattles on.

An inexhaustible subject. Because she doesn't keep to the point. An inexhaustible stream of words, because, as the wife of the parson, such talk is permitted at home and abroad but not in church. Whereas Glinski is only supposed to talk in church or at functions but nowhere else. But, as a Baptist and a church-elder, my grandfather is nearer to the true Christianity, to the honourable order of *Mulier taceat*, and thus to the true understanding of Genesis 3, and so he now enquires: Did you know, Reverend, the real reason why Adam was driven out of Paradise?

Come now, interrupts Natalie Glinski, everyone knows that, you are surely not going to ask my husband.

Well, says grandfather quite amicably, what's your opinion then Frau Glinski? And Frau Glinski knows that it was all on account of the fruits, not any old apples, as people usually think, but the fruits of the tree of knowledge. But my grandfather knows better: Well, you go and read your Bible. There are no two ways about it: Adam was driven out of Paradise—he pauses and then continues in a loud voice: because he gave heed to the voice of his wife.

Now what does Glinski do? What should he say? He must think carefully. There they are, all sitting round the long table, the Palms, old Fagin, Tethmeyer, Willuhn of course and Habedank, and grandfather spoke loudly enough. So Glinski, what are you going to say?

Glinski decides to laugh, which sounds rather forced. It was meant as a joke, after all. A bit of a nerve, all the same. At first Frau Glinski freezes. Even if grandfather is laughing, the others are not, Tethmeyer is saying in all seriousness: You live and learn!

But who is supposed to be learning here? Grandfather's intention is that it should be Glinski. At least for the next hour and a half. For now he means business, for now he wants to drag it all out into the open, clear and simple, just as he planned it. So naturally this woman must cease her chatter.

After the moment of frozen horror has passed she sees before her: Glinski, her husband, laughing, and my grandfather, insolent brute, remaining seated with his cigar, saying nothing, as though waiting for something.

Christina rushes into the breach, she heard her old man and so she hastens up to Frau Glinski and says: Little Christoph has woken up, and ushers her outside.

At last the music. And now, just before his performance Willuhn can ask for a brandy without appearing rude. Water of Life, because it helps you find the right notes, spiritual balm: because it soothes the soul, the entire being in fact, or simply brandy: because everything must be fiery. Willuhn has an endless supply of such pearls of wisdom, so Habedank interrupts: Let's give them a tune. Violin under his chin, one stroke over the strings, fine.

Old Friends, Glinski calls.

All right, Old Friends it is.

Moorland Grave, calls grandfather when they have finished.

All right, Moorland Grave it is.

Another brandy.

Tethmeyer wipes away a tear, he sighs: No, that fellow Habedank! Because Habedank always sighs so deeply when it comes to the refrain, the one about the roses in bloom.

And, with the dull drone of a heckler, Frau Palm demands:

Sabottka. Sabottka it is. In rustic four-four beat, a fine one to stamp to, a little sad towards the end.

Tethmeyer can't help himself, he joins in, in Polish. Frau Palm, the Pole, joins in too, and even Gustav's wife standing in the doorway, and of course the sister-in-law.

Polacks, mutters grandfather, but quietly, leaning over towards Glinski.

And then quite simply, he says: You are on good terms with the district magistrate, my dear Reverend, you will see that he—

Glinski interrupts: On good terms is an understatement. We were in the same student union! That should tell you enough. The fact that there is more to it, that further ties exist, is not a matter for the general public.

Now a brief *resumé* of the affair with Levin. According to my grandfather's interpretation of the facts.

I quite understand, murmurs Glinski taking another cigar. I must say that in our fight against the Polish invasion, in our position as cornerstone of our glorious empire: the laws here are totally inadequate.

Exactly, says grandfather. And so I had in mind—

You were quite right, affirms Glinski, I'll write tomorrow.

And if you could perhaps say in your letter that the case is due in Briesen on the— This music! Grandfather screams suddenly, can't you stay over there. Must you screech that thing right in my ear!

As we know Habedank is a gypsy: he has a house, but no money, a violin in a black case, a knowledge of horses—that is to say he has some horse sense, and naturally, as a gypsy, he doesn't stand still while he's playing. He wanders round the room, even through the open door to the next room, the baby might as well enjoy it too, sometimes he goes over to the round table, sings a couple of lines and then bends over to whisper a joke in someone's ear. And he has very good hearing, being a gypsy.

Glinski—the district magistrate—Briesen, he has managed to catch this much, so that's what they're up to, Habedank. If only he could hear what they are saying about the date of the trial, that would be enough. But this he cannot discover, as grandfather has started to watch him carefully and sends him away every time he approaches the table. And anyway supper is ready. Everyone re-assembles around the large table. The Palms have never left it.

Do be quiet, says Palm, for his wife has started reminiscing again: Years ago in Poland when they used to call parties Good Ideas, when they danced by candle light, the Polonaise, dances, dances and more dances, the Zauner, the Heyduck, the Lipek, such fun it was, and lasted all night.

That would just suit a silly baggage like you, mutters grandfather from the other end of the table but Aunt Wife says: Now, control yourself, you old devil, and grandfather replies: Yes, just a few finishing touches now, we're over the main hurdle. But when it goes on and on, when Tethmeyer calls over to Willuhn and waves across to Habedank, who is leaning against the hall door, hemmed in between the door frame and his violin, deep in thought, remembering some long winter or summer, but more probably a winter, when Tethmeyer calls to stir up Habedank. Just imagine in Brzésk, Matuszewicz played the flute the whole night through for his dance, because he couldn't get any musicians, and when Willuhn catches sight of the supper and the bottles which Gustav is bringing in, and cries out: Guest in your house, God in your house! this Willuhn, who is not a Pole but a German teacher, albeit no longer in service: Guest in your house, God in your house, that's what they used to say in Poland, then grandfather can no longer contain himself, then he says in a harsh, loud voice: Polack rubbish; In Poland this. In Poland that. What do you mean: In Poland they used to do this and that. For goodness sake go back to the old days and go back to Poland!

Listen, man—that is the owl Eduard, flapping his wings and staring with big, round eyes—when this was all Poland: Don't you see?

Yes, now is Tethmeyer a Pole or a German? What could he be. He makes coffins from pinewood, coffins for adults and coffins for children, black or white, seven or eight a year, there aren't so many deaths around here, and whoever needs a coffin, were he a Pole or a German, he is not particular what sort of a carpenter boxes him in. That's all the information you'll get, at least from Tethmeyer.

Jolly isn't it, this affair, says Fagin to Christina, and Christina stands up and goes out in the kitchen, there's something missing, probably salt. But Fagin gets up too and follows her, he's not giving up, he plants himself in the kitchen and starts again: Not so jolly.

What's it meant to be, returns Christina, you know what my old man wants here.

He wants to join the Protestants, replies Fagin.

No, No, says Christina, it's all because of that business with Levin's Mill.

I see, and Glinski's supposed to help. Now, what use could Glinski be? That's news to me.

But surely you know all about it, father, Levin has brought a charge against Johann in Briesen, and the old boy thinks the Germans should stick together now.

And so they must, agrees Fagin.

But what is Levin supposed to do?

Come now, says Fagin, he should clear off to Russia, and take his goods and chattels with him.

And so they talk. But what could Levin really take with him? What was swept away on the Drewenz, or the millstones? Has he anything else? Marie? If he goes back to his people with her, that will please no one, over there in Rozan. Don't worry yourself, says Fagin, your old man will wangle it somehow. You'll see. And with that he goes back to join the others. And there we see: My grandfather, between Glinski and his lady wife, exultant, uttering the most important words of the evening, the fourth sentence: Well, that's that!

Now they have all reached agreement. Glinski has not only promised the support of the local magistrate but also the court in Briesen, because Herr von Drießler is the boon companion of the District Magistrate Nebenzahl. We'll have the trial postponed. Postponed to start with. I'll see to it. I'll see to it next week. Tomorrow in fact.

That's that, said grandfather. And now the subject is closed. Habedank, calls grandfather, is that fiddle of yours ready? Yes, Willuhn replies for Habedank, just a touch of oil. So two or three more glasses and the dance gets under way.

A true Christian and a German, the Miller, says the Reverend Glinski to his Reverend Wife, and so Natalie gathers that for a while God's grace will shine forth from Neumühl. A few more words about Faith and: It would be nice if the Christians would all stick together, all the Germans, then the others would know their place, but we are making a stand, we're paving the way, setting an example, there goes old woman Palm, just like a long black bean-pole, dancing with Tethmeyer of course. We won't join them. Let's go somewhere else.

Well Gustav, how about a brandy?

Fine, says Gustav.

We've got the fourth sentence behind us and, all in all, we've made good progress: with our story of the mill that remained and is still standing, where Korrinth and Nieswandt sit about indoors or out, and the other mill which did not remain, but was broken up, at night, and swept away, this story of the Germans and the Poles and the young Jew Levin, this skinny creature, with his Marje or Marie, we've made quite good progress in this story of the Culmerland, which, by the way, could easily have happened around Osterode, but later, or around Pultusk, but then earlier, or, as far as I'm concerned, near the Wysztyter Lake or still further north, towards Lithuania, but then Glinski would be called Adomeit and Pilchowski, who now calls himself Pilch would be Wilkenies and later Wilk, which is just as Lithuanian but not so conspicuous, and Wyderski would be called Naujoks, Gonserowski Aschmutat and Urbanski Urbschies, or it could have taken place in Latvia, but then rather earlier, that's the kind of story it is. At any rate this sort of thing stirs up a lot of anger, it already has, and there will be a lot more before we've finished. But for the moment, everything is, as they say, plodding along comfortably.

Habedank has sat down by the window, the shutters are open and he's staring out, Tethmeyer is singing, Willuhn keeps fiddling with his black box and finding all the wrong knobs, the anger he suppressed earlier is starting to seethe again. That idle Palm, sitting around here, and his bean-pole of a wife, both of them, and folk have to hang around outside with their tongues hanging out, he's getting angry and makes no secret of what it is that is making him angry, and old Fagin is tottering around with a bottle, and every time he pours a glass for anyone he drinks their health in good measure, so, eventually Christina takes the bottle away from him, the Reverend's lady wife wishes to retire, and Glinski goes red in the face because he does not and she does, and Gustav's wife brings the pickled cucumbers which go so well with brandy, one dish-full after another, and, we mustn't forget my grandfather—he is somewhat tipsy. Knows he is. Should he dance? Better still! The Palm woman must dance, that prancing filly, and the sister-in-law, and Gustav, the young rascal, and not just with Frau Glinski. What is that woman giggling for? Something German, if you wouldn't mind, a Rheinländer. And what else do the Germans dance? Right: the Schieber. Grandfather is standing next to Willuhn. How did he come to be there? Just because Willuhn has pinched the bottle? On the face of it—yes, but it's not so. Grandfather wishes to make a speech, so he must stand in the middle of the floor. And what shall he say? How about:

Excellent fellow, this Glinski, such a thoroughly German man, and this woman, the lovely lady, a pure gem of a filly, this reverend lady, such a thoroughly German woman.

Something like that.

Gentlemen, says grandfather, indescribably well-disposed towards the rest of humanity, Gentlemen. He tosses his head like an ageing hack, flings wide his arms and reels against the stove. Gentlemen!

You've been knocking them back all right, says Christina taking him by the shoulders and wheeling him round to face her and then in a fierce whisper she orders: You are going to bed.

And then grandfather takes one step forward, which is not too successful, much too wobbly for the speech he wanted to make. And so he thinks: I'll stick my head in the wash basin, it'll pass, then I'll come back and tell them something, especially this fiddler fellow, gypsy and tramp that he is, and Tethmeyer and that Willuhn and old woman Palm, some Germans! I'll tell them a thing or two.

And so he lets himself be steered to the door by Christina, and beyond the door, which Christina shuts behind him, across the hall into the bedroom.

He stands still for a moment as the air is somewhat cooler here and acts like a slap in the face. First get your bearings.

On the table over there on the right next to the cupboard with the long mirror, the paraffin lamp is burning, with a low wick, so it's a nice half-light, just bright enough to find the wash basin.

There is the water-jug and grandfather says to himself: Right then Johann! and lifts up the jug and is about to fill the basin with water, when he hears a noise, there's someone there, over there by the cupboard, so grandfather turns round to face the mirror and the jug slips out of his fingers, crashes on to the floor and breaks into a thousand pieces, then someone really does come running, to see what all the noise is about.

See for yourself, there's even a second one there: a white figure, all thin and white, in just a tunic and with bare feet, or so you'd think, to see it approaching, with pearls in its hair and its breast wet with tears and still weeping, the trembling voice sighing: Krysztof, oh Krysztof.

Semi-tones of grey and white, flickers of silver, mercurial, liquid.

Krysztof, sighs the sorrowful figure and the man it has addressed replies loudly, down over his red beard: My soul. But he is not weeping.

That is Krysztof, grandfather knows immediately, Krysztof, the wild man of God, from Bobrowo, the one who hanged himself from a willow by Bialken, the Wild One, who couldn't convince his soul that it was worth while carrying on like the others, where faith was dead, burnt or driven out by Zygmut, the third of that name, the accursed Swede, that ruled here.

Oh Krysztof, sighs Krysztof's soul and Krysztof reaches for

his sword, steps towards the lake at his feet, takes a swing and throws the sword, just as it is, in the leather scabbard, so that it clatters down to the surface of the water like a wet log and sinks immediately.

Krysztof led the rebellion of 1606, the insurrection against the king, the Vasa and his Jesuits, on that occasion the Protestants got as far as Cracow, everyone knows how the king raced around the Republic calling on God. For two whole years, but all to no avail. Then the Catholics came with their armies and that was the end of the Masovian aristocracy: Catholic or exiled! A few remained at their courts and called themselves Gregor or Stanislaus, but Krysztof pressed on, to Rosenberg and Marienwerder and no one would listen, not any more. Eventually he tired of listening to his Soul, which haunted him night and day, moaning Oh Krysztof, Oh Krysztof, it stood in front of the tree, hands outstretched, and sat on the branch, all weeping spent, as Krysztof hanged himself. He seems to be coming down a hill, through tall grass his left arm is outstretched, holding off the mourning soul and he takes a great stride forwards. Krysztof, cries grandfather, deeply moved and falls to his knees, moved deeply and, with a horrible sigh, he falls on his side.

And that's how they find him, Christina and Gustav's sister-in-law, who came running to the bedroom when they heard the commotion with the water-jug. There lies grandfather, amid water and fragments of jug, in front of the mirror, half on the bedspread which he wrenched off as he fell; deeply moved, we remember. Christina goes to the table and turns up the wick, light streams into the bedroom and there we see: grandfather sleeping, his face full of tears, and as Gustav, who came in behind the women, lifts him up and carries him to bed, grandfather sighs from the depths of his sleep: Be still, my Soul! and after a while: Shut up!

After visions my grandfather sleeps especially soundly. So he has had

VISION NUMBER TWO

This time it was about Faith, about steadfast Faith, so to speak about the Union of Malken of 1874, led by my grandfather, the solving of denominational differences—Protestants, Baptists, Adventists, Methodists, Sabbatarians, Memnonites—a start has been made, for the Germans anyway, not the Catholics and Polacks.

Old soak, mumbles Christina, first he opens his big mouth too wide and now he lies flat out, fully clothed, and then has the nerve to grumble when you try to undress him.

As we see, with my grandfather, everything must work out for the best. Let's look at him again, through Christina's eyes: lying there, arms and legs outstretched, the traces of his deep emotion faded, tears dried, reconciled, at peace, and German.

CHAPTER FOUR

Now for the second or third subordinate sentence of our story. The first and possibly also the second were in chapter one, or maybe chapter two, you don't have to look far to find them. The second or third subordinate sentence is: real gypsies are really fine people.

Believe me, it's true. Although it's impossible to describe gypsies. Once I read on a church wall: Traveller, if they are strangers to you, then make them your friends, it was on an outside wall, inscribed in someone's memory.

One thing the gypsies have in common with the subject of this epitaph: they are dead and gone. Hounded together and destroyed during the years in which our story takes place, in those districts which concern us here. Where can you find them now? Whoever claims to know any is mistaken, he doesn't know what he's talking about, he is thinking of the three black-haired men, one thin and two fat, who make music in the café and do all the things which one (as an ordinary human being) expects of gypsies: like wandering around with supple joints and lithe hips, a softly penetrating gaze, a violin which sounds badly oiled and obviously has no proper middle register, accompanied by the famous cymbal. That wasn't what I had in mind. I meant gypsies that defy description, in other words Habedank and Marie and a few others.

Which brings me to the point.

Because we still have a question, something we don't know

yet: Where was Habedank this Sunday morning from ten o'clock in the morning until five o'clock in the afternoon?

He was with the Circus. There you have an answer. If you are satisfied with such a simple one. I don't think it's good enough.

So: Habedank was with the Italian Gypsy Circus. And this Italian Gypsy Circus is in the forest. Not just yesterday, and Sunday, today, but Monday too.

Monday. And the caravan door opens a couple of inches. Monday begins early: round about seven o'clock. Scarletto's head, olive skin, red eyes, topped by a greenish tuft of hair, emerges first, followed by a long neck, then one shoulder, now the door is wide open, Scarletto stands in the doorway, comes down on to the step, white, peaked hat in his right hand and says, after bowing deeply: Officer, Sir. And police constable Krolikowski replies from the saddle of his horse: Papers, work permit.

Officer, Sir, echoes Antonja.

She has come down on to the step. In Scarletto's place as he has jumped off. There she stands, Antonja, Egyptian darkness or Neapolitan night, she has the papers and hands them over to Scarletto in her pointed fingers. He leans across and takes them with a bow and says, as if in apology: If it would please you, Officer, Sir, to look at these; as he hands them up his left shoulder jerks up to his ear and his left eyebrow merges with his unruly tuft of hair, which as we said, is green.

Krolikowski takes the tattered scraps of paper in his left hand and slips the reddish sausage-like finger of his right hand into his mouth, where a wide tongue flickers over it. There are pages to be turned over, so it has to be done. But you mustn't imagine Krolikowski as podgy, he hasn't even got a beard, it's just the hands, these paws which don't seem to belong to him, he is firm, but fair, which would explain why he looks as though he had worms. A little man, constable Krolikowski, thin and peevish. But back to the papers. This little bundle. The top one is a certificate of paternity, made out to a certain Jan Marczinzyk in Lautenberg, confirmed and stamped, for a male child by the name of Joseph. So that's no good, says Krolikowski.

The next one is also no good. A dance-programme, gold-rimmed, with a little white pencil attached to the right hand side by a silk cord, from the officer's ball of some battalion of fusiliers. The next paper is a performer's permit, made out in Schönsee, last year though, but that's a start.

Then a card of honour for a mayor, torn at the bottom left hand corner, but hand-painted.

Next is a newspaper cutting, the Strasburg news, all about a tame hen, by the name of Francesca.

Finally a letter in Polish, with a printed address and headed by a large crest, where Scarletto, addressed as Pan Signor, is summoned to train certain Prince-Chartoryski rats which are at large on the estate and in the village of Krasne.

So that is no use either.

Papers, work permit, says Krolikowski.

Officer, Sir, says Antonja.

In Krasne park, behind the lake of swans, by the gingko tree, in a little round plot, in front of a green, red and yellow hedge, there is a rose, known to everyone for miles around, even if they have never set eyes on it. I only mention it because I find Antonja likes this rose.

Krolikowski looks up and blinks in astonishment. He enquires: What are you doing here?

Scarletto has a rather peculiar gait. When he moves his leg forward, he throws back the ankle with a short jerk so that the foot springs up to knee level and then recoils just as swiftly, so it reaches the ground no later than if it were a normal gait. His purpose is much the same as that of anyone setting one foot in front of the other, but the effect is different and that is to do with the fact that Scarletto is an artiste and with the responsibilities of the artiste towards the public, villagers and townsfolk alike, the latter always remaining rustic in their attendance of circus performances, for them no tight-rope act can ever take the place of a horse display, there must be horses and be it only the dullest show of dressage that a grandmother ever dashed off between her knitting. Scarletto's Italian Circus does possess a horse, but, as we see, that alone is not sufficient: Scarletto must also have a peculiar gait, it's lucky he can manage it.

What are you hopping about there for, asks Krolikowski.

We shan't answer that.

Antonja clasps the corner of her shawl, slowly descends the steps, and slowly walks through the grass to the pony, which is standing between the three trees, to which the tent-sheet is fixed, stretched out to form a roof. The fourth corner, in other words half the sheet, is hanging down and weighted with a stone, so that the sheet billows and gives shelter from the wind. There the pony is standing, beside the tame hen Francesca, it's called Emilio and instead of neighing it's inclined to snuffle. Krolikowski's horse is called Max, just once he catches a glimpse of the pony, some time ago that is, without any snuffling or neighing. But Antonja leans against Emilio, who stands there like a wooden dummy rooted to a roundabout, and says: We are artistes, Sir. And Scarletto adds: On Sunday we are performing in Neumühl. If you would care to trouble yourself to come. They're in the right there, these Italians. They'll have to be asked to produce a work permit when they are actually working, and so now won't do, and Krolikowski knows it only too well. Just a moment ago, before the ill-advised question he addressed to Scarletto, he was also curious as to what they were doing here in the forest, Antonja and Scarletto. So this is all a waste of time, no answers and no papers. Official expression, right index-finger touching helmet, a slow turn, at which Max bares his teeth.

Krolikowski rides away. Direction Drewenz. Heading for Plaskirog, nice countryside: by night cattle, by day timber, nice countryside for smugglers.

Test number one, Scarletto asks Antonja.

Test number one, answers Antonja. And Emilio nods in assent. But we don't know if Emilio isn't really from those southern shores, where a shake of the head means Yes and this nodding would mean No, as they say; that we don't know. At any rate Emilio has nodded, several times, and so we simply assume: he has adjusted himself to present circumstances, because he's a friendly sort, and perhaps we think to ourselves: it's possible that he's not from so far away after all, perhaps only Kobylka pod Warszawa or Ostrolenka or the Neuhaus farmstead, in other words a fellow countryman or fellow country-horse and so we think what we would like it to mean and say: Emilio nodded in assent.

So test number one, then breakfast. Emilio, by the way, has already been nibbling away. Right then, rehearsal. Scarletto claps his hands. Let's have a quick look at the circus-ring. Here is the caravan, a white box with a black roof, a window with shutters either side, in the back wall a door with suspended steps. And it's from there that Antonella and Antonio emerge on the signal from Scarletto, Antonio with a single leap and Antonella with two dainty steps on every rung, that is six steps in all on the stairway, and the rest on the rehearsal-ring.

That's the way it is with artistes' children, they know instinctively what to do. Antonella has a little red coverlet with a green fringe under her arm and Antonio runs under the caravan to the wooden cage and takes Casimiro by the nose.

So, in front of us on the left is the caravan, on the right, between the three trees, under the flat roof, we have Antonja and Emilio forming a group, in the middle Scarletto stands in his peaked hat and knitted tunic, and now Antonella steps forward, like a tiny flower, and says: The circus begins! and flings wide her arms, sinks in a deep curtsy and adds: Greetings from the far-off land of Italy, we begin with Number One.

You must get up again as you say the last bit, do remember child, says Antonja, don't wait till you've finished.

Antonella steps back, six paces backwards, a smaller curtsy, then sideways off and she's in the caravan again.

That's the way it always begins. The same today, Monday, in the Malken forest, in the clearing. And now it proceeds.

You must practise too, Scarletto, says Antonja, and Scarletto replies: Never mind; you should as well. But Antonja doesn't want to and anyway she can still think it over, the horse act comes last, but now: unfortunately we shall have to omit the Italian juggler Scarletto, he's not in the mood, and it's holding us up, so we'll have Number Two, Tosca's turn, the trained rat, this miracle of nature.

Antonella places the red coverlet on the bottom step, hops inside the caravan and comes out again with a little wooden cage, which she carries in front of her and puts down on the grass. Coverlet under the arm again. And now Scarletto stoops, still looking straight ahead, opens the little door and gives a short whistle and Tosca emerges, nose to the ground.

It's no good without music, says Antonio, who is old enough to join in the conversation, being ten, unlike Antonella who

63

is not allowed to yet. So the music is missing and now we realise why Habedank was in the Italian Circus, yesterday, Sunday, in the Malken Wood, between ten o'clock in the morning and five o'clock in the afternoon. So briefly, in the words of Habedank: You'll have music. Namely at the next performance, namely in Neumühl, next Sunday.

But now, unfortunately without music, the entrance of the rat Tosca.

Tosca sits up with her nose in the air, this Italian miracle of Polish nature, and is dressed up, that is, in little red pants with silver braid and a fairly wide three coloured sash round her body. First, she surveys the scene, then she moves backwards, and now sideways a little, and scratches the earth, and sniffs. But now Scarletto gives two short whistles, and she takes a couple of steps back, stops, suddenly starts to run, and, fancy that, springs into the air and does a somersault in the air, and, at this very second the red cloth with green fringes flutters and is spread out flat, Antonella does this very prettily and just at the right moment, and on this red cloth with green fringes Tosca lands, having done half a turn too many, so she comes down on her back at an angle to the spot she was meant to hit. But on the whole it's very impressive.

Now she stands and titivates her nose and whiskers and begs for her reward, and so we are quite satisfied. There's nothing to beat flying rats, you say, exactly what the spectators at the Italian Gypsy Circus usually say.

Tosca kicked her back legs says Antonio, in Phase Three. He really can join in the conversation this circus boy. But that's two mistakes she made.

So Tosca's act will have to go. The whole programme is a little shaky, for from Casimiro's cage under the caravan Francesca has kept up a constant, unbroken stream of squawking.

This wonderful hen can't wait for its entrance. It cranes its neck, flaps its wings, sinks down on to the wooden floor and emits this favourite egg-cry, which is so pleasant on the ear if one doesn't know that this very noise, this overpowering discharge of sound is Francesca's act, and by no means signifies that she has layed an egg. Francesca's squawking would suffice for seventeen eggs, but, for Francesca, there is no longer any connection between the two, either outward or inward, sometime during the day she nonchalantly drops her egg, she probably doesn't even notice it; instead, she is able to squawk: at length and with great variety, short, sharp scales, long drawn-out wails, quickly ascending into the highest ranges of smooth glissandos, she does the lot, above all without stopping for breath, stupendous. Mostly on command, sometimes, like now, out of boredom, or perhaps from stage-fright, sometimes, I think, from the sheer joy of living.

At any rate the whole programme is shaky.

I think we'll call it a day, says Antonja.

All right, says Scarletto, breakfast then.

And off he goes with his peculiar gait and his seven steps assume a particular significance. I must practise, they mean, and the others, all of us.

Casimiro, who has lifted his grey head, lets it sink back on to his paws, as Francesca has just broken off in the middle of a very high note, but his eyes remain open, that mad hen could easily start up again, in time you get suspicious.

But Casimiro can doze in peace, as Antonio is going up to the cage to release Francesca, so now she too can have her breakfast, this frenzied *chanteuse* and now we come to Casimiro's entrance.

Casimiro, let it be said, should be counted amongst the really great feats of training, for he is undeniably a wolf, *canis lupus*, there's no doubt about it, everyone recognises him, he looks like a dog, but his coat is lighter, he can only be a wolf. And now that Francesca is out quietly searching around near Emilio, Casimiro can shut his eyes, his breakfast will be along later.

CHAPTER FIVE

Habedank is already just outside Neumühl. He'll soon be home. He has learnt a song.

Very strange happenings once took place
When Moses tried to live by the water's face.

Now Habedank says farewell and the old man, with whom he has walked up the lane from the Drewenz meadows, turns away and sets his short legs to walk along the footpath. The footpath goes off to the right towards the Chaussee, the old fellow is heading for Neumühl village.

Habedank watches him. There he goes, Weiszmantel is his name, everyone knows him, he doesn't belong anywhere, he talks a confused mixture of German and Polish, his legs are wrapped in rags belted over his loins, just like a Litvak, Weiszmantel, who knows songs.

Come to Rosinske's, Sunday, Habedank calls out after him.

Off goes Weiszmantel and waves his left arm, muttering to himself.

They met in Trzianek, Wiechmann took them as far as Gronowo, then they set off on foot through the meadows and along the lane, which is shorter than The Chaussee, it cuts off the bend after Neuhof, and Habedank talked a bit about the last horse-market in Strasburg, and then about the baptism at Malken. Then Weiszmantel pricked up his ears and began the song.

Very fast waters came rushing one day,
And in their swirl they swept him away.

There he goes, old man Weiszmantel. And over there is
Pilch's house. Now evening is drawing in.
Farewell, says Habedank to himself, and now his walk
quickens, perhaps he gets that from the horses.

Goods and chattels, all he had,
No more laughter will make him glad.

Farewell, says Glinski too, we'll return to him for a moment,
sitting in his ecclesiastical office in Malken. But he uses different words, that is: he is writing it down, on paper, there—
Your faithful servant. It is the end of a letter, the previous
sentence concerned a much respected lady wife, the whole
thing started: My dear Spezi.
So this German Man of God or *Rehabeam* writes Austrian
dialect. Now he turns up the paraffin lamp as it's getting
sooty and the chimney is black at the top. And now he stands
up and goes over to the window.
He is from Galicia, and went to school in Lemberg, that's
something not many people here know, so he lived among
Austrians, together with the district magistrate who spent
his childhood with the parents of Frau Glinski. It's a small
world. Now they are both here, in the Culmerland, not
far apart, but not seeing each other very often, and both
German.
The letter is finished: To the Royal Magistrate in Briesen.
Natalie, calls Glinski, opening the door. But there is no reply.
So he goes out to close the shutters.
Which is something Habedank does not do. Here at Pilch's
house Marie does it. She is standing in front of the house,

between two mallow branches and says, as Habedank approaches: The devil's on the loose.

Show me somewhere that he's not, says Habedank. Then they go inside, where Levin is sitting at a table, head buried in his hands, Levin, who usually jumps up when anyone comes in. Habedank shoves his violin case on to the cupboard, hangs up his cap by the paraffin lamp and, says: The wick is dirty, turns it higher and then down again and sits opposite Levin: The devil's on the loose.

Where else, then, asks Levin.

In Malken, replies Habedank. And Marie puts the jug of milk on the table and says: The swine!

Yes, says Habedank, and Glinski is helping them.

But why, asks Levin, looking up, how come Glinski?

I'll tell you all about it, says Habedank. They are Germans, and that's worse than church-goers. Now Levin hears all about the Union of Malken 1874, formed on a Sunday, on the occasion of a baptism or sprinkling, between people who are not normally in unison, you might say between two different kinds of rooks, but between rooks nevertheless.

What do we do now, asks Marie. But Habedank says: Now, now and: Don't be in such a hurry, and starts talking about the Italian Gypsy Circus.

Next Sunday at Rosinke's.

Huh, at Rosinke's, says Levin with a nod and his head is in his hands again. I asked him to take me to Briesen with him next week, he's going as far as Warl. And he said: Levin, oh yes, I know all about you and your trial. You find someone else to take you.

So what, says Habedank. Business is business. Now his barn's empty. Anyway that's enough for today. Let's go to bed.

Levin gets up, looks for his cap and is about to say Good Night to Marie, when Habedank says: If you were here yesterday and the day before, you might as well stay today and tomorrow.

And the day after, says Marie.

And the day after, echoes Habedank.

He doesn't mention Weiszmantel's song.

Where was the water from on that day?
No one knows, even Moses can't say.

But Moses does know, the song is wrong there. But it will be right, next Sunday.

Marie takes the lamp off the wall and puts it by Habedank's bed and then goes out, with Levin.

It's dark in Marie's room. The buzzing of one last fly. Go to sleep, Marie tells it. In the next room Habedank is singing.

Hei hei hei hei. And again: Hei hei hei hei. Silence. Then you hear him crawling in to bed, and then one last sigh.

So you lie there and listen, there is a lot to hear in the night if you are Levin. The birds under the roof, the branch of the cherry tree scraping against the wall. Towards daybreak the wind. And the peaceful sleep of Marie. Because it's gone midnight. Sometimes dreams skim past, destination unknown, without rudder or sail.

No sleep can contain Levin's dreams.

So there he lies, eyes wide open and it all skims past: Rozan, the little town over yonder beyond the Narew. Here on the high bank, the post office, on the other side the tanneries for which the little town is renowned. The iron bridge. The synagogue, white, behind that the orchards, apple-trees, in the spring also white. The incessant humming of the bees behind Uncle Dowid's school. Uncle Dowid, white hair under his little cap and a black, black beard. He steps outside, and says:

Go on, don't delay, the sun is high already. I was sixteen then and worked with my father, even on the otter skin.

The Narew, a bit more water than the Drewenz.

They could have done with a boot-mill there.

If you play with fire you get burnt. If, if. And a lot more such phrases.

The first ray of light pierces the shutter.

Levin closes his eyes. He has forgotten how to sleep.

Now he hears Habedank sitting up in bed, and now Habedank's morning cough, much too heavy for the time of year and now the knocking against the wall and the friendly call:

Time to get up, Marie. That's all he hears, for now Levin has fallen asleep.

He's shivering, Marie says. She is standing by his bed. No, his head is cold but there's sweat on his temples.

You must wake him, Marie. Sleep simply cannot contain Levin's dreams.

There goes the last one.

Darkness. Cold. The wind hammers against the wall. The rafters creak, timbers splitting, a groaning on the sand. Water forces through the bulkhead, breaks it up. Levin jumps from the platform to the door, the wheels askew, breaking through the wall, slowly, he sees it all, the supports being washed away, the stones crashing through the floor, the roof caves in, the gangway breaks, there's wood floating on the river.

Marie, wake Levin.

The name of the devil that's on the loose hereabouts is known at least to Weiszmantel, he is just about to see him face to face. He is not really surprised, but still thinks to himself: He wasn't always like that.

But what was he like? You haven't seen him for a long time, you never had corn to be ground. If you had, you'd have taken it to Levin. You don't know how these things are, Weiszmantel: you don't know how to behave when you own something and want to hang on to it, still less do you know how it spurs you on, if you want to own more, and you have no idea at all of how it feels to be here in this country and to know: he is as German as the Emperor in Berlin and all around there are only Poles and other rabble, gypsies and Jews, and now Weiszmantel, just imagine all that coming together in one person: wanting to hang on to what you have, own more, and be better than all the others.

Grandfather comes out into the kitchen where Weiszmantel is sitting on the window-seat and Aunt Wife is re-filling his milk bowl. What are you doing in these parts, says grandfather, I didn't know you were still with us.

For God's sake, husband, says Christina, and Weiszmantel says: Yes, I'm still around, I'm one of God's miracles and I can still walk as well as Habedank.

What's that, what brings you together with that gyppo, asks grandfather.

We came from Trzianek together, says Weiszmantel, on foot from Gronowo, and Habedank is ten years younger.

From Trzianek?

Well clear off back to your precious Habedank, says grandfather and thinks, he knows what he's saying all right, and thinks, quite correctly: All tarred with the same brush.

Habedank won't have room, says Weiszmantel calmly. Now that Levin's living there.

Levin?

That is too much, Weiszmantel. For my grandfather it's just too much. His lower jaw starts to tremble, he screams: Now clear off. And calls Weiszmantel *latawiec*—a layabout or tramp. Then Christina says: Go on in man and calm down, Herr Weiszmantel was just about to leave anyway.

Herr Weiszmantel echoes grandfather with ugly, deliberate stress on each word and each syllable, and then he goes in the living-room and slams the door behind him.

And remains standing by the living-room door, waiting until Weiszmantel has emptied his bowl of milk and gone.

Then he opens the door again, pokes his head through the gap and says: Can't you see he's come straight from the Jew. Naturally Weiszmantel didn't make straight for Christina's kitchen. First he went to see Rocholl, kind regards from his Aunt and she'll be coming to the summer fair, then a visit to Feyerabend on the site, then a meal with Korrinth and Nieswandt at Rosinke's, so, in the three days that he's been in the village, he's heard and said all manner of things and now he knows more than all the rest of them put together: about what was discussed in Malken, not every detail of course, just the main gist of it, and that the Circus is coming and that the Protestant Glinski has joined forces with the Baptists.

The Reverend Feller who has dropped by three or four times now, has invited him to the rectory today. And that's where Weiszmantel is off to at the moment and grandfather is getting completely the wrong idea. When a hundred hares are drumming the ground, the hound will lose its head, race back and forth, get dizzy, yelp, and be at a total loss, then the hunter comes and says: You're no damned use at all.

That's yet another of these sentences. But as to whether it's the seventh or the ninth, there must have been that many in the meantime, or even the tenth or eleventh, I have no idea. It could just as well be the very first, or a kind of motto, or the final sentence, the simple, final sentence: You're no damned use at all.

A profitable business! Yes, indeed, preaching is a profitable business.

Weiszmantel is amazed at the sight of Feller's courtyard. The house, of course, was always there, but now it has a huge verandah with glass on the side facing the street. Instead of the open spring there is a pump in a wooden casing, freshly painted green and with a white ball on top. In the corner between the barn and the stable, which has also been extended, is a dovecote, on top of a pillar, with doors and turrets and landing-boards—a real castle indeed! There's no sign of the usual fat-arsed hens running all over the place, Feller has the finest guinea-fowls, which aren't so keen on running around, they prefer to sit on the fence all day, they don't cackle either but screech pitifully—and there's such a mess, but it still looks good. The steps are strewn with white sand, and today, a weekday, the tiled entrance-hall too, well fancy that, old Feller! And all this in the six or seven years that he's been here. What did he bring from Konojad, where he used to live! They are bound to have given him something, that crowd! I know them: Gronowski, Fellmer, and this fellow Worgitzki.

Yes, Weiszmantel knows them, they've always treated him just as my grandfather used to. They have one advantage over my grandfather, they have already heard Weiszmantel's song. Fine, today Weiszmantel is amazed, next Sunday it will be my grandfather's turn.

So Weiszmantel knocks and enters the kitchen.

A pleasant woman, the preacher's wife, born Plehwe, christian name Josepha, everyone knows straight away: Catholic family. So she took Brother Feller, who wasn't her brother at all, but she was already thirty-two then and it had to work out. Now she's no longer Catholic, but German and she's just putting away the brandy bottle in the kitchen cupboard as Weiszmantel enters.

He says: Your good health, which is quite correct.

So Josepha takes the bottle out again and sings—something not meant for Feller's ears and he doesn't hear it: Come to the Water of Life.

It seems a little strange, although not to Weiszmantel who says Good Day and: Feller said to come.

Yes of course, says Josepha, but he's not here. Then she fetches a glass and gives some to Weiszmantel, she keeps the bottle.

Drinking's best done in the kitchen. For Josepha. As the kitchen also has a tiled floor, which means you can slip off your clogs and cool your bare feet. Which lends a certain variety to the course of the conversation. When the soles of your feet are hot you talk a lot in a fairly high voice and never finish a sentence because the next one's upon you, too soon, then you suddenly see yourself doing it and cool your feet and talk in proper sentences, slow and deliberate, and the daylight wanes and the bottle too, but not your fervour, that goes on and on.

And Feller can still be a long way off.

That is a problem for Alwin Feller, in his position: his wife drinks. Really quite a drunkard already. But industrious, Weiszmantel noticed that. And they are only talking business, at which Weiszmantel is quite an expert: he travels all over the countryside with no more to his name than shirt, trousers and hat.

Yes, you have no worries, Herr Weiszmantel, says Josepha.

She puts the bottle on the table and fetches Sakuska. Cucumbers, and if there are no cucumbers, then pickled cabbage, and if there is no pickled cabbage, then pickled mushrooms, and if there are no mushrooms, then fish, jellied eels, if there are any, otherwise smoked bacon or bottled sausage or something of the sort.

But Josepha has them all, so cucumbers, and between every

bite and swig the conversation with its heights and depths, Cheers or Your Health, fast or slow.

Herr Weiszmantel, says Josepha, what do you think about guinea-fowls?

Kill 'em off, says Weiszmantel.

They lay all right, says Josepha.

Eggs are no good, says Weiszmantel. All coloured, like Easter eggs.

Quite right, this Weiszmantel. So Cheers.

And Your Health.

Now Feller arrives, we know the picture: Voice of Faith, and Gospel Songster, this time both in one hand, the left, the right hand has opened the door and is closing it again. So, Feller. The man can control his feelings, says nothing. The feelings of a preacher: he lets his head sink on to his chest, the feelings of a man: he lifts it again, he says: Wife. Mildly reproachful.

Perhaps you fancy one after all, says Josepha invitingly, just a little one. But Feller does not fancy one, and there's no more in the bottle anyway, a pity. Then Weiszmantel says: Here I am then.

Yes, so I see, Good Day, Herr Weiszmantel and I'd just like to mention one thing, Herr Weiszmantel, don't trouble yourself about all these stories, you know what I mean.

I know, I know, says Weiszmantel, *do stu piorunów*, that's nothing to do with me, damn it all! You see, says the Reverend Feller, clutching his songbooks.

But Weiszmantel must interrupt to ask: What made you think of that now?

What made Feller think of it? Well, he's just come from my grandfather. And now that the subject has been broached and everything is running smoothly, according to grandfather's plan, between confederates and school-pals and almost half-

76

cousins, there is no need for grandfather to be cautious any longer, even Feller can know all about it now, and then it will get around in the community and the pious folk won't need to gnash their teeth any more, there'll be no more secrets to ferret out and now Feller knows out of grandfather's own mouth, what is blowing in the wind.

The devil's on the loose, was one of our sentences. And so grandfather is in a good mood.

You've been talking to Habedank, says Feller.

Singing too, says Weiszmantel.

What do you mean, singing, asks Feller.

Singing, confirms Weiszmantel, just singing, quite simple.

Quite simple, says Josepha, and now there's none left.

I beg your pardon, says Feller, were you singing too?

No, says Josepha. She means the bottle.

Well, Herr Weiszmantel, would you mind stepping in here a moment. Feller opens the living-room door and goes on ahead. And Weiszmantel gets up and follows him.

Then the door closes and Josepha is alone, once again, a little red in the face, blood-pressure rather high, better sit down a moment. And inside the living room Weiszmantel is saying: It's nothing to do with me.

Quite right, says Feller.

Rozumien, says Weiszmantel, he has quite understood, as he says. But he sees things differently from Feller, namely from the opposite point of view. He is concerned with Levin and Habedank, Marie and the Circus and Feller is concerned with my grandfather and his congregation, the lack of a baptistry and the next extension, namely to his barn. So they can talk to each other at great length and as long as they don't express themselves too clearly, they'll even be in agreement, at most, wonder what it was that they had to discuss. Feller thinks: Weiszmantel won't get involved, and Weiszmantel thinks:

we'll have a fine time singing, next Sunday, but that's none of Feller's business, Habedank is bringing his violin.

So nothing more to be said. Weiszmantel takes his leave. Josepha is no longer in the kitchen, where can she be? Feller must get back to my grandfather, without delay, to tell him the news. You keep your wits about you, grandfather had said, and I'll make it worth your while. So Feller is chasing around and now we know: that lot wasn't preached together: Verandah, stable-extension, dovecote, maybe the white sand and perhaps the cucumbers, but not the bacon. How about the brandy? Josepha is singing, in the barn, in the old straw, lying there singing quietly, too quietly for Feller's ears, that's crafty—at least he'll hurry back, where can she be?

All right, says Grandfather, but what can that tramp do anyway. He means Weiszmantel.

But then Grandfather says: I'll drive out that Habedank.

That sounds ominous. Out of where? And where to?

But I think it's time we counted up the sentences so far, the main sentences. As regards the subordinate sentences, I only remember one and that was: Real gypsies are really fine people. Well then, the main sentences in their proper order. Because our narrative has become somewhat confused and the story must continue but can't do so without some sort of order: The Drewenz is a tributary in Poland.

That was the first sentence, but it was misleading.

Instead, there was a new first sentence. We remember: it wasn't quite correct, for the mill-stream which concerns us is a tributary, but of the Drewenz and not the Vistula, and so it's smaller than the Drewenz; it also said the story takes, or rather took place in a village populated predominantly by Germans. The second sentence. This concerned the Baptist minister. And told us all about Faith: this Christianity, Polish Catholics and German Protestants, although of course there were Polish Protestants, but very few, and German Catholics in rather greater numbers, if not right in the Culmerland, but more to the South or the North, and then of course the Baptists, Adventists, Sabbatarians, Methodists and Memmonites, that should suffice. The third sentence was: Yes, all right and that was spoken by Marie, Habedank's Marie or Levin's Marie, and she added: Better to stay.

Levin should stay and not go away and then the story can continue. The fourth sentence belongs to my grandfather: Well, that's that. It signifies the settlement of the Malken Union of 1874. Well, that's that. It means: The Germans will stick together, and they are, in order: my grandfather, the Reverend Glinski, the district magistrate, the district judge in Briesen, and to complete the picture: old Fagin from Brudzaw, the Reverend Lady in Malken, landlord Rosinke, and, when all is said and done, the Reverend Feller too. Not forgetting constable Krolikowski. The next sentence is: You're no damned use at all. And that, we said, was the seventh or ninth, and could quite easily be the seventh or ninth as there were several, admittedly unnumbered sentences in the meanwhile: The devil is on the loose; Germans are worse than church-goers; on Sunday we're playing in Neumühl; it's no good without music. And now the tenth sentence: I'll drive out that Habedank.

In the meantime Saturday has come round, the Saturday before this Sunday, for which Rosinke's empty barn has been cleaned up and swept out, this Saturday, which brought Scarletto's Italian Circus to Neumühl at midday, a Saturday afternoon in Pilch's house, where it is now rather crowded, eight people to start with as Willuhn has joined them, Levin arrives later, and then there are nine. And the animals. A cheerful crowd, God's blessing with Cohn says Habedank, and Marie brings round food for them all, so they can sit and

discuss whatever needs to be discussed, and Scarletto can slip
outside to practise in the evening air and Antonella too, in
Marie's room in front of the mirror on Marie's polished,
sand-strewn floors, in the lovely Saturday fragrance which
Marie has fetched from the mill-stream with a bunch of
calamus.

Calamus, this indescribable perfume: it smells of clear water,
water warmed by the sun, flowing on neither lime nor silt but
light, reddish sand, which slowly absorbs particles of earth
stirred up by the last rain, a rotting leaf and a blade of grass,
and on whose surface insects skim, such is the water it needs.
But then there is a delicate sweetness, more elusive, and behind
that, a hint of bitterness that you can't place at all. From the
earth, the soil on the bank, where the calamus roots, where it
sends out its white, yellow and pink roots, that will be from
the earth, people say, where there is some silt, as though they
are any the wiser now.

Behind the picture in Habedank's room, and in Marie's room
behind the mirror, is calamus, in finger-length sprigs, slightly
fleshier than reeds, a pretty green, lighter underneath, reddish
because it was snapped off just above the root. And in very
fine shreds it mingles with the sand on the floor. Everyone
can say how wonderful it smells, Antonella's little pointed
nose says it best of all.

It is Saturday.

So Willuhn has come too, with Scarletto and Antonella of
course, and Habedank is happy, and so he puts his bottle on
the table, just in front of Willuhn's nose: You'll have music.
Good loud music. That will be the time for Weiszmantel's
song, and he Habedank, will go on first with his violin and
swing the bow every now and again during the acts, and then
Willuhn will play, but he can sit down if he wants, as long
as he plays with plenty of bass, for, as we said: it's no good

without music. But then Weiszmantel with a good clear voice, Antonja on his right, Marie on his left with full-blooded gypsy-altos, Antonio and Antonella behind filling in the Hei hei hei heis, finally Scarletto.

It's such a pity that Francesca won't learn it, this song of Weiszmantel's, not even the Hei hei hei hei. Antonella is singing it to her, she, at any rate, mastered it straight away. Perhaps she can try again, the grown-ups have enough to talk about, and something to drink too, at least Willuhn has. Now Levin is sitting there, rather solemn, he takes his cap off and twists it in his hands and wonders what the gypsies are up to and doesn't really know the reason, he says: What are you trying to do with it all.

But who answers a question like that! Marie at any rate says: I can just see him sitting there, red all over and with eyes like Konopka.

By 'him' she means my grandfather and 'Konopka' an old Masowian mountain demon.

It's still not quite Sunday.

My grandfather should really go straight to bed for a good night's rest, but first Christina must ask him: We are going to Rosinke's tomorrow, aren't we?

To which grandfather merely replies Ho ho, and what else should he say as church-elder when his own wife forgets the Holy Sabbath. Ho ho! And: You can go if you like, I don't mind, it'll get around and then you'll see what good it does you.

The Fellers are going, answers Christina.

You surely don't believe that, says Grandfather. To that mob of gypsies!

You'll see, says Aunt Wife, Josepha told me.

Josepha yes, maybe, but not Brother Feller.

This, for my grandfather, should close the subject, but there's no chance, Christina has an idea in her head and says: You come too.

And grandfather says: I'm going to sleep now.

Sleep well.

And now it's Sunday.

Rosinke is standing at the door to the barn.

He has to stand there.

So that he knows who has arrived and who is still to come, who will fill his fine barn, how many people counting children, that is so long as there's an adult there to put something in the plate for them, the others he sends away. He will naturally charge Scarletto rent according to the number of spectators. Not according to the amount that this Italian gypsy and his Antonja and the two children receive on the plate they hold out as they go along the rows of the audience after Francesca's entrance, because everyone laughs at that, and after the horse display, because that is the climax—but before Weiszmantel's great finale, making their collection, and then again after this final song, Scarletto knows that, but not Rosinke, at any rate it's too late now.

So Rosinke stands at the entrance to the barn and keeps a look out and they all arrive, the audience and spectators, Germans and Poles, farmers and cottagers, labourers and pensioned land-owners.

Rosinke says 'Morning' or 'Good Day' and often 'God greet you' and mostly: So you've come too? and sometimes even: What do you want here? or: You clear off!

But Nieswandt and Korrinth pay no attention. Nieswandt says: Shut up. And when Rosinke hisses: Just you behave yourself here! he merely spits as he goes in and calls straight across to Christina who is sitting right at the front on the

left of my grandfather: Well, madam, come to poke your
nose in? Here they come.

Four Kaminskis, seven Tomaschowskis and Kossakowski alone,
three Barkowskis and both the Rocholls. Olga Wendehold is
already inside with that drab old Fenske from Sadlinken—
how on earth did they come to be sitting together? He's
surely not joined the Adventists? God forbid!—and old
Feyerabend from the site, and the Catholic Poles Lebrecht
and Germann with their families and, as we said, my
grandfather with Aunt Wife and, but nearer the back,
Nieswandt and Korrinth. And Christina is saying: There, you
see, what did I tell you! For the Reverend Feller is just pushing his way in behind his Josepha, who has made herself
pretty, and now he comes with his Josepha and bids my
grandfather Good Day, or rather: God greet you and Christina too, and the Rocholls, and Josepha does likewise and then
they sit down, not at the very front, but not right at the
back either, that's where the others are, the Poles, the cottagers and Nieswandt and Korrinth.

Rosinke stays at his post on the door. Scarletto goes in. The
circus-ring is naturally Rosinke's barn. The audience sit to
the right and left on planks laid over beer-barrels and saw-
trestles, supported here and there with a felling block. Beer-
barrels. How nice! So Rosinke can have some more liquid
refreshment sent over, the majority have already had a glass
or three in the bar-parlour. In the bar-parlour where now,
alone, constable Krolikowski is standing and considering when
would be the best moment to pounce.

Scarletto is standing in the middle of the barn, in his knitted
tunic, two Italian gypsy medals on his breast, peaked hat on
his head. He surveys his guests, or Rosinke's guests if you like,
but really more Scarletto's guests, I should think, as there are
some visible to Scarletto's eyes that Rosinke couldn't see.

83

Because they didn't come through the barn-door: children, for whom no one will put a coin in the plate, the ones that Rosinke turned away at the front, the ones who didn't even bother trying to get past him but crept straight in through the chaff-hold.

Now Scarletto goes up to the back door of the barn, pushes the leaves apart and lifts out the cross-beam. On the left and right Antonella and Antonja are already leaning their weight against the doors and now the barn is completely open, back and front.

Light streams in to the circus ring. Now you can see the circus caravan which has been driven up to the barn, in front Casimiro's and Francesca's cage and Tosca's little cage too, and nearby Emilio has positioned himself and, with red saddle and plaited mane, he now looks more than ever like a carousel horse. And here come Habedank and Willuhn, and Willuhn sits down with his accordion and Habedank stands opposite him and lifts his violin, waves the bow once above his head, strikes a single note, embellishes it with a flourish and plunges straight into Weiszmantel's song and Willuhn has all his fingers ready on his squeeze-box: intoxicating music, just right to sing to, for someone like Weiszmantel. Marie puts a hand over his mouth. Not yet.

The music belongs at the side, the circus-ring is empty, on the last note Antonella trips in and says: The circus begins! and flings wide her arms, sinks into her deep curtsy, starts her little welcome-speech on time and now stands there smiling at both halves of the audience, and once to the front door, at Rosinke, who has not left his post. Someone else could still arrive.

The circus has begun. The first act is due, the famous juggler Scarletto, man of many parts.

Firstly, he is an artiste, a great artiste, director of the then only circus in the Culmerland, an Italian one moreover, and then of course Antonja's husband and thus a family man, father twice over, animal-tamer or trainer, at the same time impresario in his own business as much as in family matters and those miracles of nature owned by the family, Francesca, Tosca, Casimiro and Emilio, but primarily a gypsy, even if now a somewhat unrecognizable one: the colours are too artistic, green, white and not enough red, yes, there's rather too little of the gypsy in his appearance. There he is. Proud and a little intoxicated by the size of his audience. He stands up straight, slowly raises his right hand to the middle of his forehead, takes off his peaked hat, sweeps it in an arc through the air, bowing as he does so, and lo! the act begins.

There are his seven bottles and pots, a Bohemian glass, a sort of goblet with no lid, coloured plate-glass balls and three hoops in green, white and red.

Antonio carried it all in in two baskets, unpacked it and laid it ready. Now do something with it, Scarletto! Antonio will pass you what you need. And what of Krolikowski?

Bandy-legs is still standing at the bar, Rosinke's wife gives him another brandy, the second, you must work it out roughly: he can have another four or five free, but with good intervals in between so that he stays here and doesn't disturb the performance, that would be expensive, but he mustn't become too expensive either, so good intervals in between.

I'll get that jack-in-the-box yet, thinks Krolikowski, rubs his nose with his fat paw and pushes back the empty glass. Another one already? It would be better if Rosinke's wife started a conversation now, and if nothing else will draw him out, then let's talk about Levin, this business with the mill and my grandfather, which no one mentions now, but perhaps we should: Levin wanted a lift with my husband to Briesen, did you ever hear of such a thing!

Well?

But constable, my husband doesn't get mixed up in such things.

Of course, why should he? Deep in thought Krolikowski taps his glass, surely she'll take the hint now.

But of course. And another. That's three so far. Do you know, constable, it's even going to court, whatever next! The cheek of these Jews! After all, who saw it happen?

Someone will come forward, assures Krolikowski, when it comes up before the court.

Do you really think so? asks Rosinke's wife.

Yes, Krolikowski really thinks so. Why else do courts exist at all, they must do something when they get a case, it doesn't much matter what. That's roughly what is going through his mind, and he says: When one stumbles across such a matter, one does, as an official of the law, investigate it.

But the landlord's wife has her own opinion: You and your big talk here in the bar, you can turn a blind eye to suit yourself! You're a fine one!

But in the consideration of the fact, continues Krolikowski, that the case in question is concerned with Israelites, adherents to the law of Moses.

He pauses to swallow before offering the reassuring consideration: All of which, in the present case, in the German Empire, is of no significance at all.

This Krolikowski would do better to keep to his usual way of talking: Well? or Why? or papers, work-permit.

Work permit.

Must go over there, says Krolikowski, straightening his belt, but here comes Rosine again with the bottle: Do have another, constable.

The fourth. It can't do any harm. Krolikowski, who was just

about to go, takes off his helmet, loosens his collar with two fingers and says, perched on the clay bench: There's always something going on round here, last summer the fire. . .

The performance is, I think, quite safe now. The reminiscences have started.

In the barn there was well-earned applause for rat Tosca's leap and somersault. There's nothing to beat flying rats! and: No, such a tiny animal.

The Reverend Feller expressed the feelings of everyone present: It must be a very great Lord and Master who can perform such miracles with the humbler creatures. And Weiszmantel heard, he knew that all along, he calls over to Feller pointing at Scarletto: There, haven't I always said so, he's got talent, taught her everything!

And again we've missed Scarletto's big number, but it must have been very good as Feller declines to instruct Weiszmantel on the higher significance of his words of a moment ago, he nods appreciatively in Scarletto's direction: Certainly, he is an artiste.

And now, under the arm of Antonja, the merry hen Francesca is carried in. It seems somewhat nervous, so Antonja gently scratches its chest and neck and murmurs something soothing in Italian or Polish. And the rest we don't need to describe, suffice it to say: Tears run down my grandfather's cheeks, Aunt Wife cries in delight: No, did you ever!

Today Francesca excels herself. And Scarletto is a little concerned, he hushes the audience with both hands, particularly begging the back rows to be quiet, as their noise is spurring her on to new outbursts; she finds no time at all to flap her wings. I can go a whole lot further than you, she says to herself and proceeds to squawk again, doubtless concerned with preserving the honour of her establishment, and I'm sure she succeeds.

And now the collection. And then Casimiro, presented by Antonio.

And now, before your very eyes, a real live wolf in the circus-ring. The first wolf in Rosinke's barn. Because Rosinke's farmstead is in the middle of the village, no proper wolf ventures that far, at most a miserable fox.

Casimiro stands on the threshing floor, eyes closed, it's too bright in here. Antonio leaps over his back from the right and then the left three times in succession, and then sits down in front of him on the floor. Now Casimiro slowly and cautiously places his front paws on Antonio's shoulders, points his nose in the air, howls once, tenses his muscles and springs, from his sitting position, right over Antonio's head. A fine, calm, exactly calculated spring. At such a sight your spine shivers. A man like Krolikowski goes straight for his bayonet, how fortunate that he's not there. Korrinth is the same: he feels as though he's in the middle of the forest, in the snow, and as if the moon were rising, now in broad daylight; he puts his hands on the shoulders of Feyerabend who is sitting in front of him, as though he wanted to try for himself a leap like Casimiro's, but he simply says: O Mother Poland! And it sounds like a sigh. But now more music.

A few bars very loud. And now, suddenly, softer, a couple of notes from Willuhn's box, then Habedank on his own, a melody that no one knows, with no frills and fancies, quite simple, a good one to sing to, if only someone knew the words.

And to this music Antonja rides in, black, this Egyptian Night, a white veil slung round her hair. The children at the back stand up. Old Fenske murmurs: Look at that! Froese, the knacker, clasps his face in alarm and starts to twitch his nose in all directions. The fact that Feller also secretly clutches his stringy-moustache, we just mention by the way. Josepha says immediately: My poor chest is weak. Habedank puts down the violin, he bows, he is, quite simply, proud, this gypsy.

Meanwhile Krolikowski has taken a seat, after his seventh brandy and is prattling on with a looser, freer tongue than at any other time. No more thought of circuses and work-permits, he's embarking on a story, a down-right dangerous one.

Just you keep on talking, says Rosine to herself, you won't need many more.

But the tale that the constable is telling with such fervour might be worth more than a couple of brandies, that's for Rosinke to judge, it could be useful if this fellow should get too big for his boots.

So out it comes, and from Krolikowski's own mouth, proof that this officer of the law, deals in timber across the border, and obviously has been doing so for years, as he mentions some incidents that happened way back, and with such courage and piety: Isn't it a good thing that no one knows!

My dear Herr Krolikowski, interrupts Rosinke's wife, I'd be afraid in your shoes.

At this Krolikowski can only laugh, obviously from a complete lack of fear. He, an ordinary foot-slogging constable, on horse-back, he afraid!

My dear Frau Rosinke, he cries thundering his helmet down on the table.

You and your big mouth, she thinks, finally putting away the bottle; she goes over to the window, opens it and there it goes: Hei hei hei hei. Although it can have only just begun, there are a surprising number of voices swelling the chorus: Weiszmantel's song.

Krolikowski leaps into the air as though he'd been stung, stands to attention, lifts his right hand to his temple in a salute and gets a shock as his helmet-rim's gone, he stands there, eyes wide open, knees a little shaky, remembers that it's not the Emperor's birthday, so it can only be outside, and that reminds him of the barn : the gypsy-circus, on account of which—to use Krolikowski's own words—he is here in the first place, on a Sunday, in Neumühl. So, outside officer Sir, and over there, just a minute ! What on earth ! Antonja and Marie, Weiszmantel and the children, Scarletto, in front Habedank and Willuhn.

> Where was the water from on that day,
> Nobody knows, even Moses can't say.

and

> Hei hei hei hei
> How the little Jew did cry.

There they go across the threshing floor, once each way, a proper dance, really old and Polish and with a song that gets you on your feet. Now the children at the back have joined in. Now the solo verse from the threshing-floor, Weiszmantel's tenor and the two women with their gypsy altos :

> But I thought someone had been seen,
> Late at night, by the old mill stream,

and again :

> Hei hei hei hei !

This is going a bit far, it seems to me, pronounces grandfather, it's getting positively personal. He clasps his hands in front of him, nods his head once and stands up, the Reverend Feller is pushing his way through from behind and whisper-

ing and could cheerfully speak louder, for all the notice anyone would take, at this strange Italian circus.

Enough! commands grandfather and his voice can actually
be heard on the threshing floor, and not only because he's in
the front row. But we know, it's no use.

Now, from the back rows, come Korrinth and Nieswandt, the
children Lebrecht, even Froese the knacker, a whole column
threads its way around the barn and Weiszmantel's great
song has reached its climax:

> Late at night when all men dream
> Save the good and the pious who have deeds to scheme.

Willuhn crushes his box together and rends it apart and
Habedank's violin has soared to a height from which, it seems,
it can never return.

> Hei hei hei hei
> How the little Jew did cry.

Grandfather has sprung to his feet, Tomaschowski and Kossakowski too. Feller is beside him, there they all stand in the
middle of the floor. My grandfather extraordinarily imposing,
black look, red ears.

Rosinke is spurring on Krolikowski, but he's blind drunk:
This fellow here begins to sing, hei hei hei hei! and now he
manages to mix up his legs or so it seems, but no, Krolikowski
is trying a couple of steps, as an experiment, and now did you
ever! the German constable Krolikowski is dancing towards
these gypsies, he flings wide his arms: Hei hei hei hei! And
my grandfather, with a face like a beetroot, bright red, makes
as if to bend his knees, rushes forward, and is—with Kossakowski and Tomaschowski and Kominski, Barkowski, Ragolski,
Koschorrek and everyone else of German blood, caught up in

the rhythm of the dance, which is now winding across the floor in two groups, with even steps and sudden excursions to the side at the Hei hei hei heis.

Not to mention what Francesca is offering from her cage by way of a special performance. She pokes out her head and neck as far as they'll go, between the bars, and screeches and crows and moans and rejoices.

Shall we let Casimiro howl and Emilio neigh, with a snuffle of course? It is, I think, unnecessary, but if it did occur, there would, I think, be no stopping it now.

There's no stopping any of it now. Not even my grandfather's counter-dance, which is still labouring along with its followers and, for want of inspiration sticking tongues out at the gypsy-mob and conveying obscenities with fingers, bottoms and imprecations. There's no stopping any of it.

There they stand, or rather dance: the Germans, the good and pious ones, the Baptists, who have something to show for themselves: land, goods and chattels. And in the other group just gypsies, Poles, cottagers, a sacked teacher, a couple of retired land-owners and song-lover Weiszmantel. Here, there and everywhere, staggering around, constable Krolikowski.

Levin is leaning against the barn door. How long has he been there? Once he waves to Marie. Come over here, calls Weiszmantel, but Habedank says: let him be. He sees Levin turn round and, unnoticed by the others, walk away.

They are still singing or dancing or sitting glued to their seats like Olga Wendehold. What was this performance? Was it connected with the rumours spread abroad, but quietly, that someone was seen, at night, in the spring, and that the weir water was released one morning so that all that was left of Levin's mill was half the jetty, and does it mean that there are some people who will talk about it everywhere and not forget?

What remains to be said? That the whole circus disbands into Rosinke's bar-parlour or back to the village, ʹ ʹ to the site or to Pilch's cottage.

We won't describe my grandfather's homeward path. Even Feller avoids him.

Krolikowski is sprawled out somewhere in the barn.

CHAPTER SIX

This man, my grandfather, is at any rate, in bed.

A lonely bug is crawling up the wall towards the bed.

Aunt Wife doesn't see it. But she is awake. Whatever will happen now?

Grandfather is lying on his back.

The main street of Little Zaroslo, near Strasbourg, towards Tillitz-Zaroslo, later called Rosenhain, has trees. Trees on either side, willows, many of them struck by lightning. There they stand, cleaved, some burnt out. When the air is damp, the brownish, weather-beaten scorch marks glisten like ebony. Now, in the frost, they have the dull blue shimmer of the charcoal used to heat a smoothing-iron.

It's January. The 15th of January, 1853. Not far from the broken willow, which fell across the ditch, lies a dead man. On a level with the settlement of Zgnilloblott, on the road to Tillitz-Zaroslo.

This man, a ploughman, in Tillitz, later known as Rosenhain, is lying in the road, in this snowless January, dead, his clothes completely burnt.

The jackdaws are circling. Not one of them descends. Glassy-eyed, with grey necks, they fly past. Back again. And again. On the 20th of January, the man is buried, in Tillitz-Zaroslo. On that day it snows. And in the snow stand the man's ten children, and their mother, formerly Berg. The man was sixty-one. He used to walk with a stoop. Michael, says the woman, as she drops the frozen clump of earth on the coffin's shroud of snow.

It is said of this man, found with all his clothes burnt, on the road, now long since under the earth, that he was a victim of the spirits. Nobody heard a storm on that 15th of January, 1853. It was a dead calm, they say, and the moon was on the wane. My grandfather, when confronted by this man in his dream, calls him Father.

In the dream he walks with a stoop, just as he always walked. He stops in front of a wooden wall.

This dream is

VISION NUMBER THREE

My grandfather will not be able to understand why the spirits haunt him. In the end, he will say: Not with me.

So there stands this vision Michael. In front of the wall of the barn.

And the gypsy-ghosts are swirling and screaming, scraping and squeezing out music, one shrill voice always soaring above the noise: Hei hei hei hei. Black and white faces, no other colours, just a touch of green and now and then a tiny head with a red nose which vanishes into a hand of stubby sausage-fingers. A black woman with a white bandage over one eye, rides out of the wild mob, now crushing and creaking its way across the floor, rides up to a hen that opens its beak without making a sound. And now this fellow with the rags round his legs hopping and crowing. And suddenly, with a wolf's head in his upturned hands, rushing for my grandfather. And behind him, following him, hands, nothing but hands, reaching out, with white nails, reaching out for grandfather, quite close now, clawing his clothes now, rending and ripping. And this face now, with the slothful eyes, this face, white, shadowed by water, grey and dark, and a cloud of falling rain, this narrow face with the hairy temples, Levin, this face, breathing into the face of my grandfather. It opens its mouth and says, in a voice, that is the voice of a dead man, a man found dead on the road: Johann!

Christina wakes with a start. From a brief sleep. She feels across for grandfather, but the arm, which she has managed to grasp, frees itself again immediately and punches the air, catching Christina on the elbow.

Christina's cry lifts the lid off his dream. Not with me! mutters grandfather, teeth gritted.

He lies there and opens his eyes wide. No ghosts. He clutches his breast. No clothes. Just a nightshirt. And he's not standing, but lying in bed. And so he emerges from this dream, from this third vision, unbroken: my grandfather.

Not with me.

The bug on the wall, over the bed, slept well. Now it moves off again, slowly, maybe still in the trammels of a dream. But now it has shed the dream, now it makes quicker progress down the wall. Towards grandfather's bed.

Even if I have to buy the shack, says grandfather, unclenching his teeth. And after a while he adds: I'll turf out that Habedank.

Now, taking the shortest path, and without any superfluous movement, the bug makes for my grandfather's bed.

CHAPTER SEVEN

I'll turf out that Habedank.

That's what grandfather said. A little while ago, two days in fact. And two nights.

You allow the gypsy fellow to live there and you say nothing and that's all the thanks you get!

Thanks for what?

For the fact that Habedank has lived in Pilch's cottage, up to now, in Pilch's cottage, that doesn't belong to anyone?

And: Allow him to live there?

Who has any allowing to do?

My grandfather's way of thinking is difficult to understand.

Unless you are one of his kind, or like Kossakowski and Tomaschowski.

At any rate, Kossakowski and Tomaschowski, being German, understand it quite well.

Kossakowski says to Tomaschowski: You know Ludwig, as far as I'm concerned, everyone can live as he pleases. And Tomaschowski replies: Me too. Just what I always say.

That sounds fine. And then Kossakowski says: But what's this fellow doing crawling around and opening his big mouth! And Tomaschowski says: You don't know who might come next!

So it seems that not everyone may live just as he pleases, but only as my grandfather or Kossakowski or Tomaschowski please. It's better then for the person in question. If he intends to live in peace.

Isn't that what Habedank wants? Gets himself mixed up in this business with the Jew! Which should have slipped into oblivion, but didn't. Who asked him to interfere? You don't know who might come next.

They obviously have plenty to talk about, that pair. Sitting in Rosinke's bar-parlour. Rosinke has gone to Briesen, by cart. There is a railway line, but coming from Neumühl, you don't reach it till you're seven kilometres from Briesen and by then you're two thirds of the way there, it comes from Thorn and passes Briesen in a north-easterly direction, so that's no use at all.

Rosinke's wife is standing in the doorway, she's complaining: Such a cheek, you'd never believe it, this Levin fellow, he actually wanted a lift with my husband, what do you say to that! Yes, what does one say to that? Levin used to travel with Rosinke, to Briesen or Schönsee or Strasburg, three or four times in the year that he spent in Neumühl.

What's to do with you? A pity that Weiszmantel isn't here to ask that very question.

It simply doesn't occur to the three of them here, they are completely in agreement. Kossakowski and Tomaschowski stand up and take their leave. Rosine goes back behind her clay bench.

Clear off!

It's cold outside this June. It should be harvest-time. But what is there to cut? The stuff isn't even properly green and still it must come down. Short as swine shit, grunts Tomaschowski. But that's enough of him.

More about Weiszmantel?

He's sitting in Pilch's cottage and doesn't seem to want to leave. He shall stay, as long as he likes. Sitting on the window-seat and telling his stories, his feet bare, saying Mariechen to Marie, who has his jacket on her lap and is mending the sleeve. The foot-rags and bindings are hanging outside on the line. Here Weiszmantel sits and talks.

About Schickowski, who's a good and pious man of seventy acres sand and marsh, who talks a lot, or used to, not so much now though, and not, God forbid, about goodness and piety. Weiszmantel sighs. Can you play the harmonium, Mariechen? Yes indeed, says Marie, saw it done in Kowalewo, when I was in service. Press on top and press underneath, pull those little things out and music comes.

So you don't know much about music, it's a good thing that Habedank can't hear you. Best if Weiszmantel turns a deaf ear too, he says: It's a big brown box, pinewood, a lot of music inside, every note you want.

And now more detail: On top are the stops that you pull out, high and thin and deep and thick and pretty sounding and awful as Bartholomew, all inside and works on air, which is why you have to push and shove underneath if you know how. Like Willuhn. And Schickowski, in Groß Schönau, finished, hacked it to pieces, just like that, with an axe.

Glory be, says Marie and bites the thread. The sleeves are ready. But why ever do that?

Well: The pious fellow had a dressing down from his Adventists on account of the devil's works and snares of hell, because Lenchen, who was about to get married, Schickowski's third, she had had a harmonium from her uncle in Graudenz and this thing was in the house now and the teacher came and fiddled about with it and the inn-keeper wanted to buy it and Lene Schickowski had already said: Where shall I go, what shall I do, this is the parting of the ways.

Then the Adventists came with their talk, and she could sing to her heart's content. They're coming and surrounding me! They knew the song too and shut the lid and sang unaccompanied: Flee and save yourself, you're heading for hell.

Put an end to it he did, just like in the song, the harmonium and the whole miserable business, Schickowski, with an axe, smashed it to bits, put an end to it.

But he doesn't talk any more. Now they all say, even the Adventists, that he was a fool and Lene missed her chance of a husband because of him: A bad match, and then not even a harmonium.

Such stories.

They must be nearly there, who knows, says Marie. It's past mid-day.

Marie's right. They're standing on the road, which is a main road, and so as straight as a die, the first houses of the suburb are visible, the hedges topped with lilac. They've put a good distance behind them.

Ride or walk, railway, main road, highway or by-way, all roads lead to Briesen: from Strasburg via Malken and Tillitz, from Schönsee along the railway track, from Lirrewo a straight road to the East, from Brudzaw it's probably better via Brobau and Goßlershausen than Malken and Linde, but from Neumühl you take the main road and keep to it and its northwards all the way, not across fields and meadows as Weiszmantel likes to go and Habedank too, if the truth were known, so not as if you're from Piontken or Lopatken: follow the telegraph poles

All roads lead to Briesen.

This sentence, the eleventh or thereabouts, we can write with complete satisfaction. We've got the two of them there, standing in the road, in front of them lies Briesen, 3,800 souls, the little town between two lakes, post-office, station and right next to the station the Hotel Thulewitz, horse-market twice a year, here the Struga has its source, not much more than a ditch now, later on, a little river, but deep. It runs near Falkenau, goes under the railway embankment, forms two large loops westwards in the meadows, crosses the main road at Polkau—still as straight as a die, and gradually pushes its way nearer and nearer to the Drewenz. Fifteen kilometres north-east of Gollub it comes to an end, merges quite inconspicuously with the greater, greener waters. So, we've established it passes by Falkenau.

Where the two of them have just been. You can still see them, standing there, on the left side of the road: Habedank without violin, Levin with hat. They've put a good distance behind them.

To go to Briesen you must get up early, at four o'clock if you can manage it, and breakfast well, if you can, and take some more with you. Pack your bags and go, that's the way, then you're out in the open with fresh air to breathe, it wakes you up and that's important, after all, there's a trial ahead, so you must pluck up your courage.

Habedank does this with a children's proverb: In summer there's lightning, in winter there's school, you can never stop being afraid.

During the first hour Levin says very little, Yes and No and We'll see. So they pass the reed lake, where the peewits are waking and the frogs are still asleep. A stork skims the bank, and they've reached Garczewo.

Garczewo has seven houses, but in Garczewo they found someone to give them a lift so on they go by cart towards Linde, where the main roads cross, to the left to Schönsee, to the right to Strasburg.

There are many roads, but a road's a road, however it looks and all roads lead to Briesen, you set foot on them and put one leg in front of the other, thank God, eventually someone offered a lift. As far as Polkau anyway.

Polkau has eight houses. On the left hand side are the meadows which bring the Struga to the road, guiding it to the mouth of the narrow pipe, set into the embankment, a very calm little river, with clumps of forget-me-not, on the right the range of mountains which stretches as far as Malken. Polkau has eight houses, and it is the eigth that they enter. In the eighth house lives Aunt Huse.

In this wooden house, made of round timbers, that has three rooms and five windows in all, two living-rooms and a hall, the living-rooms are higher than the rest, being on top of the potato-cellar, you get down there through a hatch. A wooden house, such as an old man and two ten-year-olds could knock up in a couple of days, even sawing the rafters and floorboards themselves, a house that sings with the night winds that surround it and sometimes leap over the thatched roof, a house that keeps warm, that no storm could break up, even if it lifted it, carried it and set it down on the ground again further on, it would still hold together, of course the potato-cellar would not have taken off. And what is man without potatoes?

From the hall to the left hand room there are two steps. Now the door opens above the steps, inwards, and reveals Aunt Huse who says: Who have you brought? What does he want?

And Habedank calls over to her: Don't imagine he needs tea! Well what does he want then? Come inside first.

So they go inside and Aunt Huse is surprised at Habedank: What's this then, no violin? and she takes off Levin's hat: Young man, what's your name?

Levin doesn't say as usual: Levin, but sits down and says: Leo is my name.

Well, what's your business, Aunt Huse asks patiently.

You know, says Habedank, it's about the mill in Neumühl.

Oh yes, Christina's mill you mean, what's the matter with it.

Plenty, says Habedank, but this fellow here, this Levin, he had a mill in Neumühl too.

First I knew of it, says Aunt Huse.

Habedank's sitting now, she's still standing, an imposing woman, large, broad in the beam, getting narrower towards the shoulders, coming to a point as it were, the narrow head crowned by a small white topknot.

Now Habedank's telling the rest of the story.

Meanwhile Aunt Huse takes a good look at this young fellow Leo, and Levin prefers to let his eyes wander round the room. He notices the proverbs, two or three on every wall, poker-work, embroidery with pearls—silver pearls on a black background—and with coloured silks: Speak the truth without fear and drink wine that is clear! Or Speak only what you can prove, drink only what you can pay! And above the armchair in the corner between the windows: We are but travellers here.

Aunt Huse has sat down in her armchair, so Levin looks into the other corner and is confronted with: Be always of good cheer!

She sits in her arm-chair, she has to. But what Habedank is saying can scarcely be borne sitting down.

So Christina's old man built a weir in the river and damned up the ponds too.

He can do that in the spring, everyone thinks he wants to trap the high water, afterwards he'll need water, when the level's gone down, there's still milling to be done then.

But not to say a word, to open the sluices at dead of night and let all the water through.

The swine, says Aunt Huse, who is not a Pole but from Gremboczin, from the forester's lodge, a German then, and formerly a Baptist.

The swine, says Aunt Huse and stands up.

Shall I come with you to Briesen?

But Aunt, what will you do there, says Habedank.

Speak up for the lad, replies Aunt Huse, he won't say a word. But now Levin does say something: It's because he has a hire-mill and mine's a sale-mill, and he adds loudly: or it was.

So what, says Aunt Huse, if you grind at your own expense, then you've also got the risk. But there's no point in telling you all this, I'm coming with you, she says and sits down again.

But you didn't see anything, protests Levin.

But I can talk, says Aunt Huse, the trial's tomorrow mid-day, I'll be there.

Now Habedank knows, her mind's made up and nothing will change it, tomorrow at mid-day Aunt Huse will be standing in the district court, in that red-brick box with the green glazed ornamental turrets. She knows exactly what she'll say, it's obvious to look at her, there'll be a scene like the one when she left the Baptists, full-blooded but dignified. On that occasion it was because of the reverend Lasch, Laschinski that was, who wouldn't allow the unmarried mothers to come into the chapel, it wasn't really anything to do with Aunt Huse and no one understood it at the time, and now it's because of the church-elder, the pious one, on whom rests the blessing of the Lord and who is trying to rid himself of his rival, in order that the visible blessings of God might rain down upon him still more plenteously.

The world is full of injustice, that's plain enough to see from Aunt Huse's window, but now the injustice is right on the doorstep, no doubt one's supposed to ignore it: up to the temple to pray, as it says, St. Luke eighteen.

No, declared Habedank and belches absent-mindedly. Amazing woman, this aunt, over seventy, but the way she sits there! Blue apron, red strings, tied on tight and smooth.

Now Levin's talking. About Habedank and Weiszmantel appearing in the Italian Gypsy Circus.

Then Aunt Huse exclaims: By Thunder! and claps her hand over her mouth, and Habedank begins Weiszmantel's song, and Aunt Huse joins in, from her chair, and keeps time with her feet, still sitting, and finds a new descant, and because her voice is really rather deeper, gets a little out of breath.

Hei hei hei hei.

Levin turns slightly pale. Habedank notices and so does Aunt Huse. What's best? Sing louder, be still merrier, isn't that right? What else can one do?

Carry on singing.

Till Aunt Huse cries: Lord save us! and claps her hand to her mouth again as she jumps to her feet. I must make you something, after all, you've been travelling since this morning.

Now comes the tea, which Habedank mentioned earlier, which wasn't supposed to be necessary. But which is good for a dozen or so illnesses, to be sure, coughing and a weak chest, ear-ache, bile, stools and ingrowing nails. And fits of depression.

The fact that this Aunt even heals broken bones with it and cures abscesses, by applying hot poultices, without cutting and so without leaving a scar, is well known in the entire district. But no one knows whose Aunt she really is. She can do everything, this aunt. Tomorrow she'll be in Briesen.

So that's what happened at Aunt Huse's. Now Habedank and Levin are on the road again and in front of them lies the little town.

Houses, houses and more houses, as if built in criss-cross patterns, cobbled streets, two church steeples, smooth stable-walls, wooden fences, tarred black. Further in the background the chimney of the König steam saw-mills, crates a speciality.

Right then, says Habedank.

And so they walk through the streets. Here and there an old man is leaning on the fence, a ginger tom-cat by his side. Already it looks like evening. They pass the market, Pehlke the baker is just shutting his shop, the door of Wiezorrek's tavern is open, German House is written over it. At the Catholic church they turn off, to the left, along Castle street towards Trench street, where Uncle Sally lives. A tiny, low, stone cottage, the *Cheder*, the Jewish school.

Uncle Sally, who was called Schlomo in Rozan, who has long been *Shammes* and janitor in other words teacher here in Briesen, flings wide his arms and embraces Levin's lanky frame, from underneath as it were, he knows what brings him here, he says: May your countenance shine forth upon your servant, and: As smoke vanishes and wax melts in the fire, so also shall evil-doers perish. Says it slowly and calmly. Then he gives Levin a hefty shove and bursts out laughing, spins round, arms akimbo and bends double with laughter. Well, Reb Jid, he says, don't you know: we are too poor for misery! Habedank has crossed the courtyard, he's sitting with Aunt Glickle in the kitchen, he stretches out his weary legs under the table. They can talk over there, we'll talk here. And Glickle sighs regretfully: You've come without your violin.

The next day, towards noon, Levin and Habedank are standing in front of the courthouse, when Wysotzki drives up in his one-horse carriage, he owns the second house in Polkau and invites Aunt Huse out. Afternoon, he says, driving on, I'll drop in at Wiezorrek's.

There the three of them stand, in front of the porch, Levin, whom the story concerns, Habedank, who has got himself involved in it, Aunt Huse, who intends to put her spoke in.

Uncle Sally wanted to come with them, but Levin thought better of it: Two of our kind and there'll be bad feeling

106

straight away. Uncle Sally just nodded and went back inside the *Cheder*, to tell the children how Ahasverus sits on his throne and laughs and sends for Esther, but then comes Mordechai with his big eyes and jet-black hair.

Now they go inside the red-brick box. Levin holds the door open, Aunt Huse strides ahead, towards the first room, knocks, clears her throat and opens the door. There sits Secretary of Justice Bonikowski, old and grey and long as a legacy lawsuit. He removes his finger from his face and says: You'll be sent for.

Why? says Aunt Huse stepping inside.

Stay outside, wait, orders Bonikowski.

We'll see about that. Aunt Huse turns round and says to the other two, standing in the doorway: Come in, close the door.

Now you've lost Bonikowski, you might as well stand up and ask what it's all about and listen to the Aunt's story and for heaven's sake don't say: How does this concern you?

But he does.

Hoho, cries Aunt Huse, concern! Your bones gurgle! Now she pours it all out just the way it seemed to her yesterday in her living-room in Polkau, everything, exactly so, and she calls a spade a spade: a German's a German, a pious man's a pious man, and a monster's both, as well as being a monster and *Parobbek*.

Then Bonikowski throws up both hands and utters the twelfth sentence: But the trial's been postponed.

Postponed? Why? Levin steps forward as Aunt Huse takes a moment to gather her senses. Mr. Secretary, he says, may I bring it to your attention that you should have notified me of this.

Exactly, interposes Aunt Huse, I should say so, well what now.

Nothing. Bonikowski sits there, old and long, notification has been given, he says.

Aunt Huse turns to Levin. You haven't heard anything, have you Leo? And then back to Bonikowski who is wondering why this woman has got herself mixed up with a Jew like that: When did you write, what did you write, above all: What sort of a carry on is this! And more in the same vein: Disgusting! and Disgraceful! and finally: Red-tapist oaf!

I'm informing you now, shouts Bonikowski.

Oh yes! you should have thought of that earlier, at the proper time and place.

Hold your tongue, commands Aunt Huse as the door to the next room is wrenched open and Judge Nebenzahl appears and says: Quiet!

Aunt Huse calmly replies: You just be quiet, I'm talking to this fellow.

So I hear, replies Nebenzahl with dignity.

Bonikowski has leapt to his feet, he lays his hands on his trouser seam and growls: District Magistrate, permit me to submit the following facts of the case.

Do be quiet, bids the old drunkard, it's about the Neumühl affair, I should think the entire house heard that.

District Magistrate, says Aunt Huse, if this is the new way of conducting your business, please save it for someone else! And now comes a dissertation on the duties of the courts, and in particular the district at Briesen—it is under your direction, I believe?—and all appropriate generalities concerning men and Christians and monsters and heathens.

Habedank is completely lost for words. This woman with the massive arse and 74 years behind her! Devil take us! He spits. But there's nothing more to be done here.

When, if you please, was the notification sent out, asks Levin.

Last week, replies Bonikowski. As you may ascertain for yourself, the accused has not presented himself.

Yes, that's true, he's not here. Where is he then? Right that's enough. We can go now. Habedank turns and stamps over to the door.

But that is by no means the end of the matter for Aunt Huse. We'll call in at the Post Office, she declares.

Yes, the notification was sent out by the court last week, the letter is at the Post Office, in Briesen. Judicial post goes every fortnight, explains the secretary. By order of the Postal Executive Marienwerder, the 17th February, 1871, figure 10, paragraph 4.

Line 2, says Aunt Huse, for goodness sake, talk like a human being!

There are no further communications for Neumühl, they discover, and so now they can really go.

My grandfather did not go to Briesen. So he must have received notification. So it worked: the Reverend's little letter, the district president's hint and the district magistrate's change of date, that's what happened, clear and simple, as if the famous ghost of Potsdam had been in attendance himself.

Aunt Huse tersely promises: I'll give that rascal a piece of my mind.

That's the thirteenth sentence: it concerns my grandfather.

A nice surprise, when Aunt Huse climbs down from the cart in Neumühl, says good-bye to Habedank and Levin in front of grandfather's house, then embraces Christina, plants a kiss on her cheek and calls her my child and finally turns to my grandfather and says in a deadly tone of voice: I've something to say to you, my lad.

There's no escape now.

And no success either. Every good soul from Malken to Briesen can talk to their heart's content, men and tongues of angels and the Lord knows what else, he will act, as we know, in the spirit of his ancestors, following their example in his usual fashion, in other words, despicably.

After only a day Aunt Huse migrates to Grandma Wendehold near the site. He's a nasty piece of work to be sure. A couple of days later she sets out on her return journey to Polkau. And my grandfather wanders around like the spirit Konopka. He rubs his hands: Because it went so well.

He scratches his neck: Why do so many people interfere? He strokes his stubbly chin and begins to mutter to himself: chuck out Habedank, get rid of the Polacks from the mill, yes and then what? When they sit in chapel on Sunday and sing: Have done, O Lord, have done, grandfather breaks off, places his hands together in front of his stomach and says in a loud voice, against the singing of the others: Yes indeed, have done now! and then, more quietly: Or I shall have to do it myself.

CHAPTER EIGHT

You get this summons and off you go, all the way to Briesen, to see them and you come back and: nothing happened! Marje, says Levin, the whole affair has been postponed, I saw it with my own eyes, all set down in writing and stamped.

But why! And how did he know in time to save himself the trouble of going, the old devil, and you didn't know, how's that?

Marje, says Levin, you don't understand.

Nor me, says Habedank.

Levin, to be sure, has had experience of such things, from a very early age, he understands, it was much the same in Rozan. You can talk about it, but what's the use?

My grandfather is going about talking to himself. He takes Feller aside, he must work a bit harder: keep his ear to the ground and his tongue busy in the right places, pouring oil on a troubled soul here and shoving fire behind a fat arse there.

I wonder what made me think of fire? muses grandfather.

He has uttered the fourteenth sentence, which was: Have done, O Lord! Or I shall have to do it myself.

The matter of the silently postponed trial date has, at any rate, spread abroad in the entire district. Grandma Wendehold says to Ragolski: I don't need such things, but you might as well do away with courts all together, if that's the way they carry on. Did the old boy, or didn't he? Of course he did, assures Ragolski.

Well then, says Olga Wendehold, at least he ought to come to some sort of an arrangement.

Arrangements cost money, points out Ragolski.

But Ragolski, he's got money.

He's got it, right enough, but that's a different thing from parting with it, he'd rather not do that.

That's the way people are talking in Neumühl, on the site, in the village, in Rosinke's tap-room. Not so Korrinth and Nieswandt, their talk is rather different, my grandfather joins them, says not a word to them for loafing again, just: Well, you two? And he sits down and says: On the fifteenth you'll be paid and then you can clear off.

Why? says Korrinth.

And where? says Nieswandt.

To Russia says my grandfather calmly. I don't need you any more.

Doing it all yourself, says Korrinth.

And what do you suppose'll happen if we don't go? asks Nieswandt.

On the fifteenth you'll be paid, says grandfather, but then you must get out.

So the two of them will think it over. Pay on the fifteenth, fine, but what happens then is by no means certain.

You can clear out too, says grandfather.

He's standing in Pilch's cottage. Habedank has good manners, he stands up. He says: Why?

Why, why, why! Grandfather is beginning to see red.

Everywhere he goes: Why, why, why?

You just go, says grandfather. And take your violin and Marie with you. And Levin, he might well add, for he knows quite well that the Jew is living here, but he doesn't say it.

Instead he says: it isn't your house.

Not yours either, says Habedank.

Belongs to Pilch, says my grandfather.

Well fetch him then, says Marie, go and look for him.

It's all the same, says grandfather, I'll get you out soon enough. And then he goes again.

This'll have to be sorted out in Briesen, he thinks to himself, it's a nuisance but it'll have to be done. If they stay here, there's no telling what will happen. So, the same trip again: to Malken!

Grandfather discovers that this Christian Union is becoming more and more expensive. He must be lavish with his purse again, but naturally the desired letter is written. The vicar's wife has come up with information. The bank clerks at Kowalewo-Schönsee insist: it's well worth it. We Germans, murmurs the parson's wife, deep in thought.

We already know what such a letter from Malken to Briesen looks like: Above My dear Spezi and below Your Servant. In between: May I bring it to your attention that this matter concerns a very influential man who is utterly devoted to our German cause.

Herr von Drießler, this 'Spezi' and district president, is in receipt of just such a letter.

All right then, quite simple: A short note to the land register office, concerning mark Neumühl, register-number 42 stroke 2, labourer's dwelling.

It is then established in the land register office: owner Pilch alias Pilchowski, settlement 1st October 1868.

Further investigation reveals: Pilchowski, Stanislaus, born 14.3.1841 Neumühl, changed his name to Pilch. The individual subsequently entered was a ploughman in Neumühl, widowed etc., reference-number 27 stroke 2 stroke 91. With the date 21.9.1868. Owner moved away six years ago. Present abode unknown. Sheer inefficiency, decides the district president in the back-room of Wiezorreks German House.

At any rate the Treasury knows and not just since today. Merely didn't notice it before. So Pilch's cottage is up for sale. Public advertisement by means of a notice in Briesen district court. Nothing further necessary, a mere formality. An interested party has presented himself. Something else nicely arranged. German appearances preserved.

Herr von Drießler answers his 'Spezi' and fellow-student union member on the 2nd of July: Once again your admirably argued espousal of the cause of our proud Empire has led me to give the appropriate direction to the consistory in Marienwerder. An application for decoration, the sympathetic consideration of which I personally guarantee, may count on authorisation from the highest quarters.

Then quite casually at the end of the letter: Superintendency Schönsee as from 1.1.75 for re-occupation.

Then Glinski repeats his wife's words about German loyalty and we already know that this is something very special to the Germans, for example the ones from Lemberg and the ones that have descended from the Polish aristocracy. Their zeal for everything German is incomprehensibly great, as we see, and their zeal for everything great is German, this too we see, in short: Germanically-great.

These people, who, according to Aunt Huse, have gurgling bones, which means approximately that their brains are dissolving. At any rate not peaceable. What they do can't be set aside with such words as Stinking lout or Swine. So my grandfather purchases Pilch's cottage from the Treasury, that's settled.

And Krolikowski will evict Habedank, officially. With official pleasure.

Krolikowski voices his plans loud and clear, in Rosinke's tap-room, but also by the fence of my grandfather's chicken-farm, he knows which side his bread's buttered and exactly how he'll stage the whole thing, it's to be a complete surprise: All of a sudden I'll be standing there in front of that hovel, high on my horse and I'll simply say: Out!

He imagines the great scene that will follow: First Habedank will come out, he'll have forgotten his cap in his fright, let's say he's got the violin with him, it's all the same to me, and then behind him that Marie with the long hair, she'll be buttoning on her skirt, and then possibly the Jew, I'll kick him up the backside, I shall just say: Here! and he'll come and I'll say: About turn, and he'll turn round and I'll kick him from where I'm sitting, and then I'll say: A song! and then they can sing, to the violin: The gypsy's life is a merry one.

Very merry. He's very good at acting out this scene and it always brings him a brandy from Kaminski or from Barkowski, but it can't go on like that. In the night of Friday to Saturday Pilch's cottage is burnt to the ground, even part of the garden fence goes with it.

And my grandfather walks around by himself. And talks to himself.

And Ragolski and Grandma Wendehold, whose conversation we overheard a little while ago, they are also solitary types. Or solitary talkers. And Rosinke the inn-keeper, who used to take Levin with him sometimes to Strasburg or Schönsee and now not to Briesen, who meanders around as it suits him, he's also a solitary type or solitary meanderer, if you prefer. And the wife of the preacher? And Christina? And, let's come back to her, Aunt Huse?

And the Rocholls. We have no wish to say any more about

Tomaschowski and Kossakowski, but perhaps we ought to: Are they solitary types too?

We could, for example, sort them according to: Who owns something? or Who owns a lot? And who owns little? or Who owns nothing at all? It's a little simple but useful, giving us several groups, many small ones, of which on closer examination, several are seen to be very similar, although they also reveal a multitude of new differences: So: The affluent or wealthy ones, who, here in Neumühl, are Baptists and furthermore, Germans, to whom the slightly less affluent ones attach themselves, and on whom folk like Feller consider themselves dependent, or the inn-keeper or traders or foot-slogging policemen, on horseback or on foot. Or teachers, as long as they are not hounded out of service, like Willuhn.

And who are aided by other solitary types: the Protestant son-of-the-devil Glinski, the Galician district president of the Prussian King, this raw as well as antiquarian monarch, who, according to a song, is a good man living in Berlin, and then district magistrate Nebenzahl, land-register office director Labudde, secretary Bonikowski, inn-keeper Wiezorrek—here it becomes more difficult.

And the other group, the one which should have consisted of Catholic Poles or Polish Catholics up to now, but which has inadvertently come to include cottagers too, and Adventists, and Baptists and somehow or other Germans too, Aunt Huse, as we have seen, even maybe Olga Wendehold, but certainly the singer Weiszmantel, the gypsy and indeed more and more people. And how about the Palms and Tethmeyer? Easy or difficult. Just the way it happened in this story. And just the way the story continues.

Habedank is sitting in Strasburg in Moses Deutsch's tavern—that is if one dare call a German House simply a tavern, he's sitting by the green stove with the pink and white flowers, sitting there with a pound of cheese in front of him, carraway-seeds and salt cutting himself one sliver after another, carefully he sprinkles them first with salt and then with carraway-seeds, as they won't stay on as long as the salt, and then he lifts a piece of cheese to his mouth, speared on the end of his knife of course. Habedank, what are you doing in Strasburg? Strasburg is a dull town, everyone says so, even the gypsies. The Strasburg horse-fairs drag on interminably. Why is it? It must be because the Strasburg district, this corner before the wide loop that the Drewenz river describes round Hoheneck and south of the plateau of lakes between Bobrau, Konajad, Ostrowitt and Pokrzidowo, does not afford its inhabitants a simple and so-to-speak comfortable existence. The woods around the lakes are very damp and become marshy to the west, to the east there's sand, on the bank of the Drewenz, to the north of the loop, there's even quicksand. It's obvious from the first glimpse of the villages. So the gypsy must be honest here and measure out his small supply of arsenic into several doses, otherwise the colt will gleam on the first market-day, but not on the third: that's why the farmers who come to the Strasburg horse-market wait until the fourth day before they buy.

Strasburg is dull. However, and we have concealed this up till now, it is really the chief town of the district. So Briesen is not at all the mighty town that we have made it out to be. 3,800 inhabitants, that's true, two churches and Wiezorrek's German House too, even König's steam saw-mills, but district-court, land register office, district president's office, that is all really intended for Strasburg. But we can't trouble ourselves about that.

In terms of its lay-out Briesen is considerably more suitable for our story if it must take place in Neumühl. And we've already mentioned that the whole thing could just as easily have happened more to the north or north-east or still further up: near Marggrabowa, and so in the district of Oletzko, or at Lake Wysztyr in the Goldap district, or still further north where a man like Glinski would really be called Adomeit and still be just as German. Nevertheless, perhaps it was necessary to admit: the main town of the district is really Strasburg, not Briesen. It was necessary but it's not important. Strasburg, as we said, is dull. Two churches, so no more than in Briesen, a saw-mill, a German House, as usual, however in addition to that there is the honey-cake factory Garczynski & Hecht and the wholesale dairy Dembowski but what good is that?

In the German House in Strasburg, in other words in Moses Deutsch's tavern, sits Habedank eating cheese. Waiting for dear old Weiszmantel, Master of the Song, with the Parezkes round his feet. Perhaps there is no need to praise Weiszmantel any more. Weiszmantel is an old man. Does one praise old people? Pensioners for example, if they live a long time and get in the way, always die very suddenly. Fortunately Weiszmantel owns nothing at all, so he's still living.

Moses Deutsch steps out of the shop, where the cow-chains hang near the soap dish and the tub of herrings, the wooden clogs, barrows, ropes and wooden churners, and enters his tap-room, skull cap on his grey head, but by no means in a kaftan, he's wearing a light suit—a merchant, he owns three houses in the market place. And for a long time he hasn't spoken to Habedank.

There sits the curate, who is new to the town—These gentlemen are always changing and never really have a penny to bless themselves with. When you see how they arrive or take their leave: a wooden case, nothing else. But strange: they arrive with nothing and all of a sudden everything that man or curate could need is there for them. So here we see the new curate sitting drinking red wine.

118

Moses Deutsch knows his way around the different grades and badges of rank, even those that are not displayed, he says: Archdeacon. If an archdeacon were sitting there, he would say Monsignor. He knows just what to say. And if this curate were the usual sort of curate he would firstly point out the mistake and then, as this makes no impression on Moses Deutsch, he would rest content. But not so this curate, he says: Herr Deutsch, I will drink my red wine at your tavern as long as I am curate, when I'm a chaplain perhaps I won't be able to any more, so 'curate' will suffice.

All right, curate it is. But why introduce this curate at all, when there are already enough characters in this ordinary story which could happen anywhere?

It covers a very wide field, so have no fear. Admittedly the largest field of all is the cemetery. Just try walking down a row of graves, here in Strasburg if you like. Everything higgledy-piggledy. Not much evidence of attempts like ours of a moment ago at grouping. Everybody sings. Rejoice, O my soul. And, as the song goes on: Grant that today with joy and peace, I may from this place depart.

With joy and peace.

How is it possible that one can just sing everything away like that? They take body, goods, honour, child and wife. Just let it all go?

Weiszmantel is there. Sitting by Habedank. Where's your violin?

Out front, replies Habedank.

Eleven o'clock then, says Weiszmantel.

So, time for two more tots.

And afterwards they wait at the cemetery.

The curate's there too. He greets Habedank and Weiszmantel like old friends.

Just look, the curate with gypsies! Remarks the mourning

widow, who must always stand at the front, to be right and proper, and now, because the company still hasn't assembled properly, is running around like a broody hen, from one heap to the next, from one group to the next, intent on striking a becoming pose at every opportunity, for whatever happens, she must stand at the front. Finally they all pray together for the next victim of death. At which point Weiszmantel silently weeps.

And afterwards there's the dividing and the inheriting and the tippling to be done. Amongst the mourners. Who can think of no more to say than: you take the three suits and the linen that's left, that'll do for you, I'll just have the loco-mobile, it's broken anyway you know.

Yes, heavens above, there'll have to be money spent on it for repairs.

That's the way it is at a funeral party.

And Weiszmantel sings his latest song.

In four-four time which starts low down and goes up a pitch every line, coming down by regular fourths within the line but still finishing up a pitch higher, not the sort of song where anyone joins in, just Habedank's violin, for which no one feels indebted to Weiszmantel:

Last boat that will carry me
Bare head, naught can tarry me
In four white oak beams
with the rue rice that gleams
My friends walk here and there
One plays the trumpet
One plays the horn
The boat's weight I can bear,
Here the voices of the band:
This one built his house on sand.

From the well the crow calls back,
From the branchless tree: alack,
From the barren stump, so bare,
Take his gift away from there,
And take from him the branch of rue,
But loud peals the trumpet
And loud peals the horn
And this not one of them will do,
They say: from time he now departs
And on his last brief journey starts.

So I know it all, and cannot wear
Another hat upon my hair
Moonlight round my beard and brow
Done for, duped to the bitter end now,
Listen once more high and low
For clear rings the trumpet
And clear rings the horn
From far away the call of the crow
I am where I am: in the sand
With the rue branch in my hand.

After each verse Habedank plays strange interludes. They're not so weird for Weiszmantel, but for us: we need words when we hear music. When the organist in church fills out one or two beats after the end of the tune with a couple of soft chords to use up all the air, the old women sing Paul Gerhardt if nothing else, well there it is under the words in the hymn book, you must have words to sing.

Let's not worry about that, Weiszmantel is just off. Habedank too.

In the coffin was Samuel Zabel, ploughman of Strasburg.

At least he is nothing to do with us, he was already dead

when we got to him. However his wife is still living, she says to Habedank: Here is your money. She points to Weiszmantel: Give him some. Habedank in fact played 'Moorland Grave', and 'Lorelei' and finally 'I know a bright jewel'.

So that's Strasburg.

Levin's voice. A fairly high voice. I've had enough, the voice says. But it's quite dark and we can't see if this Levin rubs his hand across his forehead as he says it. Quite dark.

Marie says: Stay here.

So Levin is trying to run away again.

Marje, he says and takes Marie in his arms again and draws his hands up over her thighs and presses his fingers into the small of her back and lets his head sink over her left shoulder. And presses himself against this body, so firm and soft, as if to drown in this heavy, throbbing breath, in these long and sudden swift sighs, in these unexpected bursts of stifled laughter, in this hard embrace, in the swelling sweetness with its aftermath of salt: like the light which suddenly penetrates gloom in bright shafts: planks where the joints are light, not daylight yet, but: light, dawnlight, four-o'clock-light.

At this hour my grandfather lies swathed in the white frock of innocence.

Christina is awake. She hears the regulator. To and fro. It has just struck. I won't ask any more questions, says Christina and closes her eyes. But she cannot sleep.

Pilch's cottage. Four rooms. Thatched roof. Pilchowski's people used to live there.

Habedank has gone. Marie too. Someone's prowling round the house. Unseen.

He's panting a little. Although he's taking careful, measured steps. He grasps the shutters. They give at his touch but he goes on, round the house. Now he stops still.

A strange wind. A steady stiff breeze. But all of a sudden it starts to hop and skip. As though trees had got in its way. Yet there's not a single tree in the meadows. Not even a crooked willow like the ones in paddocks.

Perhaps it doesn't want to come over here, this wind off the river. But with all its leaps and starts it's here now. And it catches the little fire at the corner of the house and sends the baby flames searing up the wall, and higher now, and to the roof. And now the old wood burns, the brittle straw doesn't flare, it smokes a little, smoulders, then burns brighter and brighter, first the one gable, then roof and rafters, finally the whole house.

With a hum which stays at a constant pitch, sometimes loud, sometimes soft. Burns to the ground. It finally flickers away at the fence. It charred a couple of posts and palings, and licks the next one now before it dies.

My God, says Christina, when grandfather rolls into bed. At three o'clock.

Aunt Wife, enquires grandfather.

But Christina is silent.

My grandfather falls asleep immediately.

We'll have to clear out, says Marie shaking Levin by the shoulder. Yes, I know, says Levin and sinks back into his sleep. So Marie remains lying there. It's getting light in Rocholl's barn, the one by The Chaussee, just before Gronowo. The strong smell of fresh hay makes you dizzy. Almost like being in a fermenting vat.

There's so much sneaking around, thinks Marie. Perhaps I should go with him, into the Russian zone, to Rozan. Like Levin says. But I know, thinks Marie, how it would turn out! Levin stops short when he's started to talk about it. I know, those are his people, I don't belong there.

I can see them all standing there. The old men with their

iron-grey beards, the women with white pasty faces and black burning eyes. They'll say: Where have you come from now, Levin? And Who's that with you? And they'll turn away. I don't belong there.

But Levin must stay here with me, says Marie. He must stay, here with us.

Between Gronowo and Trizianek, half a kilometre to the north of the Chaussee, lies a little wood.

A beech-wood, one of many in the district, copper-beech, *fagus silvatica*. It's not really a proper woodland district here. Average yearly rainfall less than 500 millimetres. The larger tree crops, fir, *picea*, mainly *picea excelsa*, spruce, are by Dombrowker and towards Schönsee and then in the north, round Goßlershausen. Here, half a kilometre to the north of the Chaussee a field-track leads to the little beech wood and then becomes a wood-track. And when you've gone a longish stretch down the wood-track and the light from the fields gets nearer and nearer, under the broad beeches, slow and quiet, you come to a house. In this house lives Jan Marcin. The owner since it was built.

He is supposed to be Scarletto's father, no one knows but everyone says so, and he owns a couple of goats with brown, striped backs and black hens and a coloured cock. He always lives here and the others in his house are only visiting.

There's always someone there. The shady element, as Police Officer Krolikowski says or stubbornly imagines to himself, and so he's always calling by, on Max the gelding, and not once has he found what he's looking for, farm workers on the run from Ciborz or poachers or lone smugglers. You always find the others here, difficult to understand why it's always the others; some staying a long time, others passing through, some just poking their nose in the door, never the ones that Krolikowski wants, the ones that make themselves quite comfortable there, but are of no interest to him, such strange guests too, like the ones who have been staying with Jan Marcin for two days now.

They only come into the house for a couple of hours at night, and then only towards morning when it's getting cold. Otherwise they roam around, lie at the edge of the wood, run to the Struga and dangle their legs in the water and come out with two bunches of forget-me-not, using their mouths for everything but talking. Jan Marcin doesn't mind, anyway he doesn't say anything, except: They could put something on. He places the clothes, blouse and skirt, jacket and trousers and two linen shirts, which he finds simply thrown across the bed, on the bench at the foot of the bed. And whistles. Strange people.

Marie milks the goats and Levin downs half the milk straight away, and then they're off again, sometimes you hear them somewhere, but they're never there. Now they're sitting in the meadow and it's raining. It's the time when you hear the oriole, especially at the spot when the copper beeches finish and the silver beeches start, *carpinus betulus*. He sings you into a trance with his pealing voice, you listen and listen and your eyes grow dim, and if you are old, like Jan Marcin, you lean against a tree and move your lips, but say nothing, except perhaps: My life.

You can even hear the oriole from across the meadow. But now it's raining and he ceases his song. And Levin and Marie are sitting in the meadow in the rain, with nothing on, just shouting: There, there, there, and again: There, there. They are counting raindrops, each one counting those that land on the other.

It's still raining slowly. The drops still seem to turn to spray on the glowing bodies. You scarcely see them land when they burst and disappear, without a trace. But now it's raining more quickly, still in drops though. So the counting gets quicker and louder, a real din, and now Marie's hair is straggled across her face in black, wet strands. She pushes herself up, kneels in front of Levin, who's still lying on his side, waving his arm in the air. She runs both hands through her hair, gathers it together, lifts it over her temples to the back of her head, holds it in both hands behind her neck and squeezes it so that the water runs down her back between the shoulder-blades. As she does so her shoulders tilt back and her body curves forward under her breasts. What's the matter, says Marie.

Yes, what's the matter with Levin?

There he lies on his side, and heaves himself up out of the grass a little with his right hand. There's something to see in Marie's lap, something for Levin to see. For the raindrops are swiftly falling one after the other down on to Marie's tuft, they cling, swirl, run down the tiny hairs and pull them downwards with their weight, the tuft lies flat. But here and there one or two pop up, now another simply won't stay flat. It's funny, Levin laughs—And Marie says: What is the matter with you? She's still holding her hair.

What can Levin say? It's nice here in the meadow. It's nice here in the rain. When was it last so nice?

Before the rain, around mid-day, old Jan Marcin potters around in his cottage, on the worn floors, he straightens the patchwork quilts, pinches the blackened wick off the tallow candle and pulls a contemptuous face. First one, then another, then another. With the third he stands at the window.

From the Chaussee and along the wood-track comes foot-slogging policeman Krolikowski on horseback. Jan Marcin pulls a fourth face. Now Krolikowski stops in front of the house and calls down from his horse: Come out here! Just as Jan Marcin appears in the doorway.

Krolikowski is surprised as always, this time even more than usual: the old man is alone. He dismounts, takes the three steps to the door, the old man stands aside, Krolikowski goes through the two rooms, he doesn't even notice the clothes on the bench, he goes outside, he sees nothing at all, mounts again and quickly rides away. Jan Marcin remains standing in the doorway, watching him go. And when the two of them return to the house, long after the rain, he says nothing. Krolikowski had just left when the rain came on. Perhaps just to wash away this horseman's tracks, thinks Jan Marcin. Why should I say anything!

I live, says this Leo Levin, for the first time.

They are sitting in the living-room, the three of them, Jan Marcin is telling a few stories. Such tiny fragments. About Lea Goldkron, who ran about all over the place with bare feet, and wherever she went with her red hair, the manors burnt. The one that the old prince, up in the Rypin district —there was a summer palace up there where he lived—the one he had captured on account of her beauty. Lea who went into the lake, years after that, with all her clothes and jewels on as far as the shore and then took everything off on the sand, and in, just as the day she was born, naked. But old now and with weary legs.

When he's finished, you can hear the crickets again. Here inside the room. They are in the moss caulking the walls. Once Levin suggested taking the old moss out and putting in new. But Jan Marcin shook his head.

Now Levin understands why. He stands up, goes to the middle of the room. He declares: I don't want to leave here. Marie has sunk her face into her hands, she says from behind her hands: Tomorrow we'll go home.

CHAPTER NINE

The fifteenth sentence does not belong to our plot. Although it does to us, it is approximately: The sins of the fathers shall be visited upon the children to the third and fourth generation.

Here we are talking about fathers and grandfathers and we must realise that these fathers or grandfathers were just as much children themselves of the third or fourth or twenty-seventh generation. There's no end to it, once we start looking around. We find sinners upon sinners that hold us up and meanwhile maybe, we silently withdraw.

Although, for example, this whole story is being told on our behalf.

Dear fellow, fare thee well, these words may be found in Albert's Musical Composition of 1641, which, as we gather from the title, reminds us of human frailty, which we try to forget. Weiszmantel is not familiar with this Königsbergish Song although it's very good, sung with three voices, un-accompanied or with instruments, with lovely words. But he says it exactly the same as this Herr Albert: Dear fellow, fare thee well. And Habedank says: Well then, let's be on our ways. But Weiszmantel prefers to tag along a little further as far as the top of the hillock before Neumühl.

The pair of them have just come from the Drewenz meadows again, the same as before. The Strasburg burial is forgotten and the new curate too, they are talking about horses, about a grey mare from Kladrub in Bohemia. Strange, the way an animal like that gets around! She was in Cielenta for a while and foaled the following year in Rosenhain, now she's in Brudzaw and she's already been sold to Linde.

And the two of them have reached the top of the hillock. And Weiszmantel does not say it again: Fare thee well. He stands there and says nothing. Like Habedank.

Over there, on the spot where Pilch's cottage stood, for thirty or forty years, stands constable Krolikowski, nothing else, only a piece of fence. Krolikowski has placed his right hand in the uniform jacket, two hands' breadth below the collar. There he stands and now Habedank goes up to this policeman. And Weiszmantel stays where he is. Officer, says Habedank. Shut your trap, says Krolikowski and then corrects himself in accordance with his official capacity: You hold your tongue. So here, on the charred remains of Pilch's cottage, Habedank is arrested, in the name of the law, by this fellow Krolikowski. And is brought to Briesen. And the testimony of Weiszmantel, of no fixed abode, is summarily rejected. By Krolikowski. Arson, declares Secretary Bonikowski and Judge Nebenzahl says: Adequate suspicion.

So, admitted by the district prison at Briesen. One unavoidable procedure: Questioning, directed at the police sergeant in Strasburg, of the following content: Whether the prisoner, as testified, personally participated in the burial (catholic) of Samuel Zabel, ploughman of Strasburg. Together with an individual by the name of Weiszmantel. If seen in Strasburg, when and for how long?

We know that for those who love God, all things work out for the best. The Reverend Feller has just said so, in Neumühl, in my grandfather's front parlour. My grandfather replies: True indeed, you see it happen time and time again.

Amen, says the Reverend Feller, which means: So be it.

It already is, concludes my grandfather.

That will do for the sixteenth sentence.

Yes, mutters Feller to himself. What did I get so excited about? It all turned out all right. He did go to Malken but so what! The Jew's gone, there's no mention of a trial, the gypsy's in prison.

That's all he knows, and that's enough.

And my grandfather sends Aunt Wife out to the scene of his own crime. And then they stand up and lift their glasses to the window and see the pleasant afternoon light shining through the clear liquid. This was a day to remember. Everything turned out perfectly, says Grandfather now I don't need to buy the shack. Bound to have been lightning, says Feller accepting a second brandy and: Krolikowski took that particular flash of lightning away, and now he's locked up.

After the third brandy it's: The prayer of the righteous man prevails. And after the fourth brandy judgement is pronounced on the whole affair: it was God's own judgement, without a doubt: the Right of the Lord has been victorious. You can preach a sermon on that next Sunday, suggests my grandfather.

I'll do that, says Alwin Feller. And with that he goes home. And finds his house empty. And goes through barn and stable calling into every corner, softly: Josepha, and realises Josepha is out.

I'll wait here, he says in the kitchen, but he doesn't wait long after all. Goes hither and thither and Josepha has already been everywhere before him, but has been gone some time now.

I can't repeat the things she was saying, says Barkowski and Rocholl asks straight out: Did she get it from you? Rosinke looks at him sideways: You never come here otherwise, is something the matter? And Tomaschowski says: I'd be careful, if I were you, Brother Feller.

So Josepha Feller is running around all over the village. Now she's at the site. They are at Froese the knacker's place: Grandma Wendehold and Feyerabend, sullen old Fenske from Sadlinken and Germann the Pole, and Josepha Feller is spilling a few truths: The old boy did it.

Even if he did, says Fenske, who can prove it?

Just like the other time with Levin's mill, says Olga Wendehold. Sitting in front of her cards again, and she frowns and scratches her top-knot with the corner of the queen of clubs. To hell with it, says Feyerabend, slamming his cap on the table, and it'll just go on and on, I suppose? And your old man's in it too?

Josepha, it must be admitted, is not drunk enough to get over that. She leaves the bottle on the table and rushes home. And arrives at her beautiful farm. And sees standing in the doorway, Feller. Who, for the first time, loses control. His teeth grit back the cry surging up inside him. He lifts the Voice of Faith and with it strikes Josepha in the face. And now the second cry comes, it won't be held back, it rises up over the new roof and the fences.

The third one does, however, fall back in his throat. He throws aside the book, he clasps his face, he sees: Josepha has turned away and is walking slowly out of the gate and slowly down the village street and slowly into the dusk.

Run after her, drag her back by the hair?

But perhaps no one saw.

With that, he goes inside: The innocent have much to bear. He means himself.

But Habedank is in Briesen. Sitting on a wooden plank. With no violin. He gave it to Weiszmantel, he'll look after it. Marie and Levin will be well on their way now, past Garczewo, they'll have reached Polkau before dark.

The mist of the Struga meadows is seeping up to the road. So it should, after such a day. The ridge of hills stretching eastwards to the Struga is still dimly visible, it's still a little brighter than the meadows at its feet, it's still catching some light. But a lone star has already appeared. And there's the croaking from the reed-ponds to the west.

It takes a lot to worry your father, says Levin.

I know, says Marie, but Lord, this time maybe.

Maybe? Because Habedank is tired, not so good on his feet any more, no better than Weiszmantel, and he's getting on. But there again, maybe not? As a gypsy. Even here, in clink, as they say in Briesen, in this official box which is a square, tile-red building stitched up with iron bars, where from the inside, you have no idea that the *ksiezyc* or *la lune* is rising, this very minute: the he-moon or the she-moon, and now someone who remembers should say: the gypsy's sun: as the *ksiezyc* or *la lune* rose over the forests, white and round and strange as water, when the fires died down and dwindled away on the earth, when the wonderfully dressed robbers came down from their mountains, ahead of their brocaded girls, who had captured them with silver mounted belts, cloths and embroidered or gaily woven ribbons. Then the maidens came striding down and sang aloud, and the robbers heard it and were afraid no more.

Here too, where you can't see the *ksiezyc* or *la lune*, where it just gets dark, much darker than outside, so that only the high barred window, this tiny criss-crossed opening lets in a meagre shaft of light, even here Habedank isn't worried, a real gypsy, who has a violin and knows more than anyone else about evening and night.

He sits there, legs dangling, ready to talk, and to be silent too, he is not alone in this clink, not even alone in this cell, there are three others there, one is young and the others are about forty. They are telling stories and that suits Habedank. For months now he has only been able to talk about things that everyone knows anyway, and these three know nothing. Nothing about the mill, neither Levin's nor my grandfather's mill, nothing about Krolikowski and Pilch's cottage. In fact, nothing at all. The young fellow at least knows something about Neumühl: where it is. He was once in Gollub. A boot-mill on the Drewenz, he says.

But it wasn't a boot-mill, neither this one nor the other, and not on the Drewenz river at all. The whole story must be told in detail.

It's a tributary of the Drewenz, a fairly fast one, on the right bank there are two weir pools belonging to the big water-mill. Which stands, or rests firmly on twenty-four posts, supported and propped up with supports and props, and covered with lead against ice. The mill has a large undershot wheel and a first-class grinder and there's plenty of work for two men there. And now, as far as I know, the old boy has kicked out the two of them. But they haven't gone yet. But the other mill that one's small, put up in a hurry last year. Levin is from Rozan and managed to learn something about milling and set up this mill right away, down river. Just four posts and boards and planks and a light wheel, as the water's quite flat and the shack swayed rather a lot and so he attached two chains and anchored it against the current, the mill lasted through the winter and into the spring, it's unbelievable really. And he did good business.

A Jew like that, says the young fellow, arrives with a bare arse and does business.

How's that! Less of the bare arse. He came with money. Bought every plank, carried them by cart from Gollub. I made dowels and later the planking, two days—everything finished.

And first of all no one came.

But why? asks one of Habedank's listeners, the one with the

134

goatee-beard, who gave the cavalry captain a thrashing in Wiezorrek's German House, that old soak Herr von Lojewski. There he had sat, this one time cavalry captain, loud-mouthed, protesting that German beer is thrown away on Polacks and that it's no longer an honour if they can buy German beer for the same money as decent folk, that it simply can't be true, that they can loaf about all over the place, these Polacks, like sand in the sea.

So this fellow with the goatee-beard gave him a thrashing, not a very thorough one, and twisted off one of his medals and left him with its imprint on his bald head, because it was a bit tarnished, perhaps it's all cooled down now. Anyway that's why he's sitting here.

But why make such a fuss about a Yid, says the goatee-beard, come on now! And the other one, who hasn't uttered a word so far, puts in his spoke. One of those who don't talk much, but when they do, it's rubbish. These Jews, he says, they nailed Jesus to the cross, with nails, eight inchers. He knows all about it. Now they are running around over the whole world, he says, marked like Cain as the murderers of Jesus.

That's all so familiar now, that it seems like the truth.

And that's the way he said it, the one who normally doesn't talk much, his voice was quite calm, without a trace of emotion. He knows his facts, he won't harm a single one of these Jews on that account, he won't anticipate the works of God, who is faithful and who will take his own action, as it says in Thessalonians I, and when he does take action, he, who doesn't normally talk much, will stand there, and not be surprised, it had to happen, he might just step a little closer and maybe lend a helping hand.

The young lad has heard all this before of course, so it must be right, but there again it can't be right. When I was in Gollub, he says, there was a Jew there, an aged little man, they used to carry him around on a chair, from morning till evening people used to hang around him wherever he went, there were no more trials in Gollub for the half-year that he was there, they went to him with all their problems. Who knows where he is now?

The three men say nothing. And the lad thinks, he wouldn't have been any use to me. For he was a drover and sold a cow that wasn't his, in Lissewo, and it was discovered straight away. He would have needed someone with money.

This Levin, you say, he came with money?

And a cart, says Habedank.

And what then?

Well, what then, says Habedank. He bought and milled corn and sold flour.

And the old boy, who milled for a fee in the usual fashion, he saw how suddenly some folk began to sell their corn to Levin, as ready money was scarce, it had been so bad that they paid their taxes with swine, because they had no money. And the old boy's eyes grew wide at what he saw and he wandered around cursing all the time and once he said that he was going to show the Jew—he didn't say what.

And in the spring, one morning, all of a sudden, Levin's mill was gone. Only the jetty was left and the two posts that held the chains.

Well, how on earth. . . ! The man with the goatee-beard has pushed himself up off the bench and is leaning against the wall. And the other one, the silent one is also maybe not thinking that a miracle took place, for he asks how it happened.

This silent fellow is only here, by the way, because someone else stole some wood, at the König sawmills, it wasn't him, and certainly not at König's.

Well, the water came, says Habedank. You could see what must have happened. The ponds were drained, and in front of the big mill the old boy had built a weir, the water had been right up to the edge, and in front of it, down river, it was so flat that the sand was sticking out. And so this weir was torn up. And it didn't happen by itself. Anyone could see that.

But who would do such a thing, says the lad.

Who indeed? Goatee-beard grins. And what did the Jew say to that?

Took it to court. In Briesen.

And now?

And now Habedank tells the whole story: about the date of the trial in Briesen. About the Italian Circus in Neumühl. About Pilch's cottage.

Meanwhile night draws in. At eleven o'clock the guard comes to the door and says: You might be quiet now. And stays by the door listening. Until this gyppo's story has reached Briesen for the second time. Right, that'll do for now, tomorrow is another day.

As though that means anything!

During this night Aunt Huse doesn't sleep. She has lain down but she doesn't sleep. Levin had to tell her everything, where he's from and how he happened to come to Neumühl and get mixed up with my grandfather. And Marie: What happened with Pilch's cottage, how they came along the Chaussee and how the house should have come into sight but there was nothing but hard flat sky.

I won't come with you, children, says Aunt Huse the next morning. You go alone. It isn't worth it, it'll all clear itself up in a trice. It must.

Habedank really was in Strasburg, he didn't leave till the morning of the day before the fire. An old woman will know, in a little village south of the Malken forest, a farmer too, a younger man, who was driving a rack wagon in the Struga meadows and took two men along with him, one of whom had a violin and the other sang to himself all the way. He took them quite a long way. But who will ask them?

Everyone knows too how far it is from Strasburg to Neumühl. But that's why Habedank is still just a gyppo and always will be. No, there's no reason why it should clear itself up in a trice. The night is over. The guard has brought in acorn-coffee. And there the four of them sit.

The lad has started up again about the story Habedank was telling the day before. Who were you with in Strasburg? Weiszmantel? And he sings all the while? What does he sing? Sing us something?

Habedank doesn't want to sing. So the quiet one sings, just sort of by the way. The guard honoured him with an extra good morning a moment ago, he has, as it transpires, already been here several times, he's practically a permanent resident.

In the clink at Briesen
You come in through the door,
There's lice and your feet start freezin'
But there'll be a whole lot more.

And then: Wum-ta wum-ta wum-ta wum-ta. Quite simple. One to join in with.

Habedank is used to better songs. Yes, if only he had the violin here to put some life into this dreary sing-song! This is no good. What can possibly come next?

Out of the clink at Briesen
You go out through the door,
Take your lice and feet still freezin'

Till you come back again for more.
Wumta, wum-ta wum-ta wum-ta.

That's all. The repeats don't make it any better. Wumta, wum-ta wum-ta. No better at all.

Meanwhile Habedank is learning something new.

Goatee-beard started it yesterday towards evening. When the flies had given up dancing under the low ceiling, making only a few more buzzing criss-cross flights, and finally one after the other hung themselves on the cell-wall and, after crawling around a little, stopped still, and when the fat bluebottle had come to rest, the one that had only agitated up in the tiny window space, periodically battering his hard head against the pane.

Goatee-beard had said: There, you see, flies? How ever many flies together, that's the number of days we're stuck here.

Everyone gets the idea immediately.

So: There's a fly. Higher up, exactly above it, a second. Here comes a third, settling just under the first. Three already. But now the topmost fly flies away again. Is it coming back? Does it count if it's flown away again. What's the rule, must they stay still?

Here comes another fly. This one lands a couple of feet above the spot where the top one was. How many is that now: three or four? Thank goodness, here comes the other fly back again! At any rate it lands exactly on the spot just vacated. So that's definitely four.

What if one were to shoo them away? Would that mean freedom today? Out through the door, wum-ta wum-ta? No, better not, sixteen might come in their place, four is better than sixteen in this case.

But what if one swatted these four against the wall. Then there'd be four and no more. That would be an achievement.

You've no idea at all, says goatee-beard. How many do you imagine would come to the funeral!

Wum-ta wum-ta wum-ta.

And anyway dead ones don't count. Otherwise you could catch some and stick them on.

He's right there. And so the oracle proceeds. But naturally there are little tricks.

If only one had some syrup. Or sugar. If need be, it will even work with spit. One damp smear drawn on the wall, with a finger, they'll settle on it. Even when it's dry. No one could tell. But not with baccy, says the expert. So: When the spit tastes of chewing-tobacco the flies don't like it. No tobacco at all.

Here comes a fifth fly, but this one crawls over to the right again. Perhaps it's turning round?

Everyone's eyes are glued to the wall. Even now, in the morning, when it's light and the flies prefer to flit about over the mens' heads and only seldom does one of them land on the wall. They sit and stare at the bare plaster. Will it settle or not? Will another one come?

Towards mid-day the flies calm down for a while.

Four days? Five days? Sixteen?

No, there's no reason why it should sort itself out in a trice. Aunt Huse is wrong there. Her picture of the world is too rosy.

Of course the world should be much better, even Aunt Huse admits that, but it's worse than she imagines.

A visitor for Habedank? Who? His daughter?

And what do you want, young man, are you a relative too? This is a new fashion, a visitor !

You'd better go to the district court, there round the corner.

Room one. There's a fellow there with a red nose. And mind your manners in there. Be polite and refined. And say thank you. Quite a new fashion. Gaoler Szczesny has been on the job for twenty years now. Military service before that. But he can't recollect a visitor. It's never happened before!

Even Bonikowski is surprised. A visitor?

Just a moment, weren't you here a short while ago? Mixed up in this Neumühl affair, yes, the water-mill. And now you're here again. On Neumühl business again. What do want?

To visit someone, yes, understand?

What is your relationship with the prisoner? You're not related at all. Well then, what is it you want here?

Yes, and are you trying to have me believe that you are the daughter? We get so many, you know.

And so it goes on, back and forth. Until finally: Very sorry, out of the question. You would have to prove your identity. Or bring witnesses. Impartial ones.

In criminal cases, but these people, gypsies, Jews—can't understand that kind of thing, what is it called: Aiding escape? Danger of obscuration? Something like that. At any rate: Conveying information. *Kassiber.* Possibly in code. Maybe by sign-language.

So no visitors.

They both go to Uncle. Two roads, up the square, the narrow alley.

Uncle is holding his lessons. Aunt isn't at home. Perhaps she's with a neighbour. I'll go and see, says Marie and runs outside.

Leo Levin sits with his back to the wall and listens through the thin wall, to the voices in the next room. The shrill ones, sometimes mingling in. Confusion, quick and slow, and then the deep dark one following everything up and taking care to carry all the others along as though with a guiding hand on their shoulders, keeping pace with the shorter steps of the quick voices. You can't hear much, at any rate no words or sentences. Levin stands up and goes to the door. And he can hear more.

As I've told you: when there's an accident, don't you go running up, you just stay nice and still and don't go near. But scream, scream as loud as you can! Others will come, others who can help.

So, now Levin is disappointed. Just listen to that, he says to Marie, who is just returning, she hasn't found Aunt. Perhaps she ran past her, not knowing her. But none of the people she had asked had seen Aunt. So, just listen to that.

Uncle is explaining it all again.

Don't go near. But scream, scream! Others will help.

Why, Levin? That's quite right! Suppose someone's lying under a horse and the little children come, the horse will still kick with its three good legs, only the fourth is broken. Or it will bite. There you are, you see.

And now Aunt does appear. Stands in the doorway and says: My Leo. And looks at Marie and says: Leo, who is that.

That is my betrothed, Marie, says Levin.

Uij uij. This Aunt is somewhat startled.

Marie retreats a step, white to the roots of her hair. And suddenly laughs, very quietly.

It's not true, he's joking. I'm Habedank's daughter. The one with the violin.

Oh, him, yes, he was here, I know him, says Aunt.

Now add: that he's locked up here in Briesen, this familiar Habedank.

Uij uij, child, says the Aunt. But she's still not reassured. Leo's betrothed. That wouldn't do at all.

In the next room Uncle Sally is dismissing his children. The shrieks penetrate the whole house, up the garret-stairs and down again into the kitchen. Uncle Sally is standing at the door, waving his arms. When the children reach the street, they are quite quiet.

No, there's no reason why it should clear itself up in a trice. In Strasburg, the chief of police goes by the name of Birfacker. Nobody knows where he's from, he just appeared one day, he's still a stranger here, perhaps he'll go away again some day. Now he has received a letter. From the district judge at Briesen: Arson, the suspect had made illegal use of of the property in question, probably an act of revenge, eviction was imminent.

And then there's a passage in the letter concerning my grandfather: he is a German, living at Neumühl. And a passage covering the (extremely) suspect Habedank, imprisoned at Briesen, the district gaol: that he is insisting on the interrogation of the new curate by the name of Rogalla.

We'll summon him here, says Birfacker.

And so the clergyman arrives. Praised be Jesus Christ. Birfacker, growling: 'Day. So the curate takes a seat without a word. I have summoned you here, growls Birfacker.

I know, says curate Rogalla.

I beg your pardon.

You have summoned me here, says Rogalla, and here I am.

Not so simple, this fellow. As a precautionary measure, Birfacker says: I hear you're still quite new. You won't know your way around as yet.

Oh indeed I do, says Rogalla, already I've done four funerals, three holy baptisms and one marriage, it doesn't take long to settle in.

Would you mind listening to what I have to say.

143

So now for Birfacker. We need the whole of this conversation.

Sir.

Curate, corrects Rogalla.

Yes, says Birfacker.

You, like myself by the way, are not from these parts, I take it.

Oh indeed I am, says Rogalla, Rogowker, 22 kilometres from here.

And you.

No, I'm not. It doesn't matter anyway.

A short pause. After a growl: You are, my dear curate, undoubtedly aware of the responsibilities of your position.

Our Holy Church, says Rogalla.

Our German Empire, corrects Birfacker. Embodied for us all in the venerable person of our heroic Emperor.

And what have you in store for today, asks curate Rogalla.

I'm just coming to that, growls Birfacker. So: Property number 42/2, Neumühl, belonging to the state treasury, proprietor until 1 October, '68 Pilch, let me finish, is, as a result of arson, to be regarded as a total loss, if you please curate, the suspect, a gypsy by the name of Habedank—do you know the man by any chance?

Habedank, considers Rogalla.

So you don't know him, Birfacker immediately establishes.

I'm still thinking, says Rogalla.

He could really go home now, thinks Birfacker.

Who is this Habedank, asks Rogalla.

Travelling musician. Says he played at a funeral here in Strasburg.

Yes, I remember, says Rogalla. Burial of Zabel, Samuel, violin, oldish man. There was another fellow with him, he sang. Nice people.

Curate, says Birfacker, it is really totally immaterial who played and sang, or indeed if anyone did at all. It's quite customary and nobody bothers themselves with names and so forth.

But you did ask, says Rogalla.

Mere formality, replies police chief Birfacker.

What makes you think you know a vagabond gypsy, of all people?

I'm afraid I don't understand, says Rogalla.

You will understand in just one moment, curate. This vagabond gypsy inhabited a property in Neumühl which did not belong to him. The purchaser of this property had ordered him to vacate the same. Whereupon, this gypsy, vindictive like all gypsies, set fire to the property.

So you know all this, says Rogalla.

Well yes, the facts are known. But this gypsy maintains he was not in Neumühl at the time of the fire, but in Strasburg. That could be right according to the date of the funeral, in other words : the fire was started in the night of the following day.

It's three days from Strasburg to Neumühl. I wouldn't say that, curate. Good horses, a change in Malken : a night and a day.

Improbable, I agree, but still quite possible.

Chief of Police, says curate Rogalla, we can eliminate that possibility. That man, or rather: those two old men.

Curate says Birfacker, rising to his feet, you surely don't intend to protect this rabble, which is such a problem to our administration? What good would it do you?

Is that a question?

Yes, curate, I would ask you to answer that very question.

It's fairly dark in this office. Cramped too. On the window-ledge there are four plates of fly-poison, but it's probably too inhospitable here for flies.

The document-stand near the writing-desk is crowned by a bottle.

Red wine, says Birfacker at the curate's glance. Known to you in several respects, no doubt.

Our Holy Church, begins Rogalla.

Never mind that for the moment, interrupts Birfacker, this is a matter of national importance.

Then I can go, says Rogalla.

Please remain.

Chief of Police, says Rogalla, I have the impression that you are conducting a cross-examination here.

Nonsense, says Birfacker and immediately assumes a more friendly tone. He wipes his hand across the table and does find a fly between his fingers, he looks at it for a while before continuing.

Let's not beat about the bush, he says, squashing the fly between his thumb and index finger. This is a clear case of a vindictive act directed against a much-respected German and thereby against the entire German people, you do understand me?

No, says curate Rogalla.

Birfacker raises one hand and holds it flat between himself and the priest. Now listen! If we, as Germans, have a duty, then— The curate looks at Birfacker from under raised eyebrows. I'm not at all sure about that. Good Heavens! Birfacker has snatched at the paper-weight and now flings the thing, a piece of shrapnel from 1870, on the floor.

Rogalla has risen to his feet. I am certainly superfluous here.

We've been through all this before, what's the point of arguing.

But now Birfacker is on his feet too. He says: You should consider that aspect, curate. We are here as Germans. I would have thought you would have understood that.

I am a priest.

I know, curate, a German priest. Your church authorities would have very little sympathy for your indecisive attitude.

Chief of Police, says curate Rogalla, if I might ask you to reveal to me, in plain and simple terms, exactly what you want. I will consider the matter.

Consider, growls Birfacker. Trapped again. Perhaps it was unnecessary, back there.

Well, curate, we need your testimony. It has been requested by the District Judge in Briesen and is required there. Will you be able to testify under oath that this gypsy—

I don't think you are really in a position to put such a question, what was your name again.

Birfacker, Chief of Police, and you have misunderstood me. Naturally I am not entitled to demand that you take an oath, others will do that. I am asking whether you say this itinerant gypsy by the name of Habedank, here in Strasburg, at the time in question. No evasions please, we need an appropriate testimony.

Now Rogalla must think again. He remains standing. After a while he says: On the day before the fire, if the date of the fire is correct, he was here, in Strasburg, I saw him again in the evening about eight o'clock. An elderly man. His companion was obviously older still. I also remember seeing both of them before the burial in the German House—

I'm not interested in beforehand, interrupts Birfacker.

So the desired testimony is not to be had in the most desirable form. We will have to keep an eye on this clergyman, Birfacker resolves.

147

Good, according to your testimony, on the day of the fire this Habedank was no longer here.

I can't say, replies Rogalla, I didn't see him again but it would be nonsense to imagine that those two old men could have taken themselves off in the night just to set fire to some shanty.

He says shanty, this priest, so he really is from round here.

But Birfacker must interrupt again: Do not minimise this occurrence, from my own experience I have permitted myself to describe to you how it must be regarded.

After a short pause: I'll have your testimony written out. You will be good enough to confirm it with your signature. Schimanski! And there it is, signed by curate Rogalla, who had to take a lesson in German behaviour, who is to watch his step in future, who is none too sure of the support of his superiors: Habedank was here until the day before the fire, up to eight o'clock in the evening. That's all.

Whether or not he returned to Neumühl, says Birfacker, in a day and a night or the other way round, I don't know and you don't know, and it is not ours to decide. A curt bow, Birfacker opens the door and calls down the dark corridor: Schimanski! completely blind to the nod with which curate Rogalla leaves the office. Schimanski!

Here comes Schimanski!

Here, with a letter to Briesen, district court.

So the testimony is sent off. And takes its time. From Strasburg to Briesen. Police post travels slightly faster than judicial post, as directed by the postal executive, Marienwerder.

But our Habedank still has ten days in gaol behind him when he is taken before Nebenzahl.

Ah now, there you are, says Nebenzahl amicably. You can sit down, if you like.

I don't know says Habedank.

No, you don't know, but we know all right, says Nebenzahl. It isn't too bad, the old hut is burnt down that's what all the fuss is about!

But how do I come to be inside then, asks Habedank.

You must tell the truth, you know, says Nebenzahl, you did set fire to it.

And because Habedank lifts up his hands immediately and cries: But oh no, he adds calmly, as before: Perhaps you were baking yourself a hedgehog and the hut went up in flames with it?

Could that be it?

Let it be said for anyone who doesn't know, hedgehogs are baked rolled in clay. When the ball of clay, which is simply placed in the fire, is hard and cracks, it's taken out and split open and the skin and prickles remain stuck in the clay. But gut it first. You can stuff it with potatoes if you like.

I wasn't baking a hedgehog, says Habedank. I came back from Strasburg, with Weiszmantel, and Pilch's cottage was gone, Krolikowski was there.

You came from Strasburg by cart, isn't that right? asks Nebenzahl.

A little way by cart, but not much, no one came along. Patiently, Nebenzahl questions on but nothing further emerges. The two old men walked, on their legs. That's the way it was. I'll speak to the District President tomorrow thinks Nebenzahl and sends Habedank back to his cell.

The conversation with the District President is short. Herr von Drießler has other worries, he must see to the evening's bowling.

You will come too, Nebenzahl? No ladies this time I thought, more informal. And this arson, you surely agree, it's not worth getting excited about. Settle it in the land-register and that's that!

It's different in the courts, remarks Nebenzahl. The Chief of Police in Strasburg thinks it's an anti-German action.

But my dear fellow, says Herr von Drießler, where would that get us? And Nebenzahl can't help suspecting that it's one more case of typical Austrian inefficiency.

So my grandfather receives the notification from Briesen: Sale of Property No. 42/2 Neumühl, labourer's cottage, not possible, as the same was burnt to the ground.

And what about Habedank?

Four days later Habedank returns to Neumühl. With Marie and Levin.

Dear Grandfather, it wasn't quite enough this time. Suspicion alone was not enough. No evidence could be brought. No evidence in this whole business.

No evidence.

CHAPTER TEN

Habedank is roaming about again, even in Neumühl. Perhaps that is one of the so-called subordinate sentences that we weren't counting; a subordinate sentence because it lacks two of the characteristics of a main sentence: striking brevity and, most of all, feeling.

Although the content of this subordinate sentence is quite enough to set mouths working, and heart and gall too.

It affects the heart of Weiszmantel and, of course, Marie and Levin. Not forgetting Aunt Huse, who took him in on the way back from Briesen and gave him a bunch of flowers as he left, love-lies-a-bleeding, which is good for diarrhoea. Olga Wendehold and Feyerabend have come to welcome Habedank back, and Weiszmantel has brought his friend his violin, that's best of all.

Habedank is sitting outside of knacker Froese's front door, on the green bench without a back, plucking one string after another and listening to the fading sounds; as the notes match themselves, in turn, to the shrill cries ringing down from the roof, and recede, reasserting themselves, but gently, just before they die away.

The swallows bombard the roof with a quiver of cries, where their nests cleave to the top of the wall, these hemispheres of beak-white, laboriously collected clay. And because the edge of the roof on Froese's house projects a good way beyond the wall, there is always the little downwards swoop just before the nest, with no reduction in speed of course, the deviation, a kind of dive and then immediately afterwards the steep upward flight to the edge of the nest, to the semi-circular opening where the wide beaks of the little ones are open in loud wails.

That is something for Habedank's violin: The top E-string vibrates to the cries of the little swallows, the others, the A- and D-string, and towards evening the deeper, fourth string, echo the soothing twitterings of the parent birds. And when Habedank lets his fingers wander over the instrument, sometimes swiftly, and then again slower, a strange musical dialogue can be heard, those songs of few notes, understood by the herds in the fields and every shepherd in the world, interrupted by a lilting trill, and then again the clear notes, still clear as they fade away. You close your eyes and feel on your eyelids the current of air that the swallows bring, you listen, the cries have ceased for a moment, but there it is again, just as loud, only the one baby swallow was quiet for a moment longer than the others, it had a greenfly and now it's crying again. Habedank digs his toes into the sand. He too has his eyes closed. He lets his violin drop and leans against the warm house wall. In front of him, in Froese's overgrown garden, the hawthorn is still blossoming, it goes right to your heart. Like another deep breath, but one for which you had waited long.

Your hearts are touched. So is my grandfather's gall.

The gyppo released, he says, his mouth twisted. In fact that's all he does say. And Aunt Wife does not pursue the subject. Feller's wife has been staying with her for a few days now, looking after the hens and starting to bottle the goosebeeries. They must have plenty to talk about. At any rate Aunt Wife turns Feller away at the door.

Most of the day my grandfather is in the mill, where it's time for repairs and the mill stones to be examined. When all the corn is threshed and stored in the granary the mill must be ready for use. There'll be more corn and work coming in before the year is finished.

The Polacks are still in the village. Perhaps I should fetch them back? In the meantime, who knows—but the main thing is the Jew has gone. No one will be in such a hurry to build another mill in front of grandfather's nose. But, as we said, it troubles my grandfather's gall. And this trial still isn't over, there'll be another date, not straight away, I'm sure, but before the end of this month of July.

What more is there for Glinski? My grandfather has entered everything tidily in the back of his Bible. A pretty long list. Right, let's get that done. That's what my grandfather says. Perhaps that was a seventeenth sentence.

Herr Nolte, Frederick Nolte, Chief Administrator at Neumühl, is an old man. We haven't mentioned him so far because he has been confined to his bed all this time, but we'll disturb him now, we'll let him get up, with seven deep sighs and one long groan. As he sits down in his underpants at the desk where dust has collected and the ink dried out. He finds his note book and opens it. And muses for a long time and snaps it shut. How is one supposed to write up something like that? Even if one had ink. And one would only have to dissolve the dried out mass with a little water. How is one supposed to write it up.

Chief Administrator Nolte sighs and rubs his right leg and sighs again and suddenly comes out with the eighteenth sentence. Troubled times! What does Herr Nolte mean by this. Is he perhaps referring to Pilch's cottage?

Troubled times, Nolte said and he means worse troubles than that. Something is always burning down, usually barns. No one is safe from lightning or that kind of Pole. And of course full barns burn more easily than empty ones. And insured ones better than uninsured ones. Everybody at the fire insurance in Marienwerder is just as well aware of that as here. And is not particularly bothered. If someone has worked it all out so that a stable must burn down before he can recover and build himself a bigger one with two more cows in it than before, then there are probably rumours in Marienwerder too: Don't you think someone helped the Good Lord with that bonfire? But they are not particularly bothered. A short report from Chief Administrator Nolte, that's all that is required. So it's not Pilch's cottage!

Naturally, anyone else but this Habedank, could have sat there in Briesen for at least a year and a half, till he was black in the face, any other Pole or gypsy, one who hadn't found a curate, or at least not one with a good memory. Troubled times, Chief Administrator had said. And firstly he means that trouble has been stirred up in the village of Neumühl and still more trouble at the site. So much trouble at the site. So much trouble that it reached his sick bed.

The Reverend Feller was there. Nolte already knew that Josepha had left him. But he said nothing, and neither did Feller, they only spoke about the troubles: the fact that Nieswandt and Korrinth have been sitting around in Rosinke's tavern recently, because my grandfather payed them off. But there are others too, Feyerabend, Lebrecht, and the like. They can just clear off, those two, Feller had said. So: Nieswandt and Korrinth are supposed to disappear.

He's actually right there. Anyone who can't prove that he's working, anyone who 'is not in a position' to do so, as a Pole or anything else, has no right to remain, according to the regulation concerning immigration and residence of persons of foreign nationality of both sexes, of October 1st 1863. Additional decree of the previous year. Although that is not enough: foreign nationality. There are others, as we said.

And then Froese the knacker, was there. Because Albert Kaminski went over Froese's head and simply buried the dead heifer. Now there are no very clear regulations about that, and Froese is really concerned about something else, namely all the troubles. Only he's not talking about Nieswandt and Korrinth, but about Levin's mill and Pilch's cottage. In a round about fashion, as is Froese's way, for he can't fall out with anyone in his profession.

And finally news was quick to reach Nolte's ears of what took place in Rosinke's barn: this circus.

Troubled times.

Chief Administrator Nolte sighs again aloud and says: When Krolikowski comes by again I must have a word with him. But constable Krolikowski doesn't come by, neither the day before yesterday, nor yesterday, nor today. Where is Krolikowski keeping himself. Nolte's aged landlady asks around in the village every day, and comes back—the day before yesterday, yesterday, today—and says: He's not there.

Holy Mother of God, exclaims Korrinth, whom the old woman has met on the road to the site, what do you want with him?

Herr Nolte wants to speak to him.

Korrinth refrains from spitting, he whistles through his teeth. And swings round and says: I haven't seen him, and is in a hurry to get back to the site.

If you see him, give him the message, Nolte's landlady shouts after him.

Of course.

I don't know, I really don't! Nolte's landlady stands there, arms akimbo: He's supposed to come, that Krolikowski, and he just doesn't turn up.

Where is Krolikowski? That's also one of those subordinate

sentences, but we won't delay over that one. We'll simply cross the Drewenz, by Plaskirog landing stage, a little further up river is the ford.

Krolikowski came this way too, with his duty horse Max, but without his uniform, in other words without his bayonet and official cap, in civilian togs, to use his own words, four days ago now, by night.

Through the ford. Through the forest. Round the marsh. The next village is called Walka. Just before Walka on the right hand side in the meadows stands a barn. He came this far on horseback, unseen, he knows when the border guards make their patrols. But the right people weren't there, not at all the ones that Krolikowski had expected, they ought to have been there, but it was the others who were there.

Then Krolikowski did a lot of talking, in Polish, a lot more quickly than usual, and flung his arms about and cried out and finally fell on to his knees with his hands in the air. But they pulled him up by his hands and layed him over a tree trunk and beat him with clubs. Because they were the wrong smugglers, not their rivals Krolikowski's smugglers. They took down his trousers and chased him across the fields to the wood straight into the marshes. See how you get out of there. They kept the horse Max.

Now what is Krolikowski thinking. Up to his knees in the marsh. With every movement he makes he sinks a little deeper into the damp slush.

O dark night, when will you be gone?

He could try singing that, this Krolikowski, but he was never pious and didn't learn it. And who knows if he would sing anyway. He could be crying out now. But he's not.

In all probability he's afraid of the Russian border guards. He hears the one bird screeching intermittently. He hears an animal prowling along the moor. In search of moorhens. Which don't come here.

The moon remains quite still in the same spot. You can't see if it's getting deeper or paler. It remains quite still and moves on no further.

Every now and again the gurgling of the marsh. No other sound. Now he does start to cry out, but who's likely to be running around here, apart from the smugglers.

In the morning just as he recognises the birches in the distance, his smugglers come by, on their way back from the border. And hear him calling. And get him out, quite easily, with felled brushwood.

He was stuck chest-deep in the marsh, he probably struck an old tree trunk, something firm at any rate, which stopped him from sinking in any further.

He's shaking, although the marsh is warm, they have to support him. And the whole affair has turned him so silly that he starts chattering about the Russian, Innskentij, the leader of the other smugglers, the enemy.

So that's where you were, you scoundrel. That's why there were no signals. That's why we had to throw the goods in to the water.

Stani, the wild one, who was always so obliging, nods his head to the right. Towards the three oaks.

Stani's men are in a hurry, it's light already. When they ride on, one stays behind. One who is hanging from the tree. From the furthermost branch of the left oak tree. The dirty clothes are spread out on the grass to dry. It's all the same to Krolikowski who takes them next day.

I want to see Krolikowski, Chief Administrator Nolte had said. He's not there, Nolte's aged landlady replies for another couple of days.

No one will ever discover why he didn't come when he was sent for. He has vanished for good. Years later a white bearded merchant who had set up business in Strasburg is heard to mention a German policeman, one evening he suddenly says: He was hanging from a tree near Walka, saw it with my own eyes, from an oak. The old fellow refrains from mentioning that he hung him up there, with his own hands. And why should he?

Nolte opens his book again. He enters as much as he intends reporting, but not the whole story. Tomorrow, maybe, he'll be better. Then he'll go to Rosinke's.

As Rosinke will have to withdraw his report. What's the point now: Krolikowski's smuggling activities. Who the devil will care now. Book shut. Finished.

The new policeman is called Adam.

Now the right sort are coming, says my grandfather. Adam? That's a proper Polack.

A story with no evidence. A story with no motives?

Why, for example, did Rosinke put in a report.

That's something we don't know.

Perhaps because Krolikowski had accustomed himself to standing around in Rosinke's bar-parlour. And demanding brandies, on the house of course, throwing out dark hints.

What sort of hints?

That's something else we don't know.

What will my grandfather do: If Habedank continues to let his violin sing in and around Neumühl: Hei hei hei hei. If Weiszmantel, the wanderer with the rags around his legs, finally restricts his wanderings to a to and fro between the Neumühl site and Jan Marcin's cottage in the wood. If Nieswandt and Korrinth sit or stand around every evening by Rosinke's bench and drink, on my grandfather's money but not to his health. If Josepha Feller continues to stay and

158

haunt him in his own house as the living reproof or the stern-faced warning, not drinking, silent when my grandfather is in the house, but talking for sure as soon as he is out of the door. Leave me in peace, you bums, says my grandfather, grabs a piece of paper and goes out to the shit-house. For the last time today. It's dark already.

The comely wooden construction is reached by a path framed with white tiles and raked only today, between lilac bushes and black alder trees. Where the alley-way ends, two juniper trees flank the door and wooden step in front.

The building is a solid piece of work and typically German, built by the same travelling Polish carpenter that erected Feller's dovecote with all its landing boards and its pointed roof.

Unfortunately my grandfather interrupted him at the time, in Polish, but the gist of what he was saying was totally German, all about simplicity and size, and so, unfortunately, the entire beauty of the conception never came to fruition, the pentice on two columns with its dog-toothed frieze is missing, as are the two balustrades. It could have been more beautiful, but it's still beautiful enough.

There is, by the way, seating accommodation for two, with no dividing wall, so it's possible to go in twos and hold a conversation without having to talk through a wall. But my grandfather is alone.

He stops in front of the door, looks right, then left, then over his shoulder and even behind the privy, which is another name for the little house, and he makes a careful inspection, he's had a nasty experience, and he listens for a while before he turns the lock, opens the door, goes in and ceremoniously takes a seat, the one on the right, as is his wont. His caution is well-founded.

Although the detachable box under the seat is hidden by a

flap suspended on two leather straps, this flap made of cross-boards has crevices, through which one can comfortably stick a piece of wood sloping downwards into the substance inside, manure or so-called human-cow-dung, so that the longer end of the piece of wood juts outwards, and in passing, this can be comfortably trodden on, so that the shorter end springs up against the occupant. You can get a nasty shock like that, it's by no means customary, more of a surprise really. Two weeks ago it happened to my grandfather.

At any rate his pride forbade him to mention it, except to Christina of course, who must share joy and sorrow, as woman and wife and Aunt Wife.

So there he sits. Still not quite at ease. And it's dark too. Ghosts and such like could easily come.

That's why my grandfather left the door open.

The local nightingales are singing from the little mill-stream behind the village, thrush-nightingales. Their song carries as far as here and my grandfather might well listen to it, but who knows, perhaps that too would irritate his gall, now that he sees himself surrounded by enemies: Catholic Poles and Polish Jews and Jewish gypsies—here he means Marie—and gypsy Italians and who knows what else.

But he hears nothing. At most the rustle of a dry twig falling to the ground perhaps because the crows over there in the pine trees behind the cowshed are having a good sweep out before settling down on their sleeping perches.

So, nothing but a rustling.

All lights in the house turned off.

Stars perhaps.

My grandfather, whilst relieving himself, considers between the plops: What is to be done.

And then he takes the paper he brought with him, which is incidentally, the notification from Briesen of the unsale-

ability of a burnt down shack by the name of Pilch's cottage.
With a quiet grunt, because he has to lean forward.
Now he could really get up, but he remains seated there.
Now, I think, he even hears the nightingales. At any rate
he closes his eyes and leans back slowly.
What peace!
My grandfather's soul migrates. To the site. And he says to
himself: If you don't drop this business . . . I'll get the lot
of you.
Should one tell him now, in this brief moment of peace, that
he over-estimates himself?

CHAPTER ELEVEN

Come, come, come.

Scarcely anything. The cooing of a dove. The screeching of a cat. The hoarse, shrill whinny of the young stallion: as he draws back his narrow head from the rack; something stirred behind him, at the stable door, yet it doesn't open.

Plonek, thinks Ofka, shivering, half-asleep, he's skimming the roofs, red-eyed, in the skin of a ginger tom-cat, trailing his fire-tail of death-cries behind him.

Little chicken, says Jastrzemb, little chicken, come. Wild days. A glow like fire. The night rises with lights that sweep the heavens with their wide, plunging trails.

Jescha, the heathen God, and the others, Pomian, Swist Powist have long been talking over the wall, sitting on the earth mound, talking to the old house-spirit Chowaniec, who comes in now, between the two door-hinges and springs up into the rafters. They've gone now, the night is over, a night like a yew-tree, which scattered the tiny, sharp-pointed lightnings of early dawn, like little flames again and again till it exploded darkness, swirling, a shadow-swan.

The morning is bright. No one knows how it can be morning after a night that one missed: always getting up, going to the window, to the dormer-hatch, pushing back the heavy shutters, over and over again.

The moon has described a white line, a thin semi-circle in the sky. Lelum and Poleum have raced ahead of him, the brother-stars as the Byzantines call them, the Dioskuri.

Here the sleeping woman lay, one arm under her head, under

the hair that covered her shoulders, a wave frozen. To hear the steady breath in silence, the flicker that troubled the temple, flying away soundlessly, the vein rising over the breast, subsiding and returning.

Come, little chicken, come.

Ofka flings back her arm and starts up with a cry. The man is bending over her, gently settling her back on the pillow. And in his ears the far off call of the horn, just audible after Ofka's cry, is still ringing.

Old Strzegonia. Returning early. We should have ridden away yesterday.

The girl emerges from her sleep.

Your father, says Jastrzemb.

But the thought again: Four days to ourselves, they're over now but nothing can take them away.

Now the signal is nearer, three horns. Now the hammering on the door. Swords.

Strange spirits that have discovered my grandfather here, through the open door.

He has fallen on his side, he stirs, he murmurs: O Lelum. We'll fill in a few details without knowing how my grandfather has stumbled upon this Jastrzemb, this the oldest of his forefathers, who found favour with Boleslaw, the Chrobry, apparently because of the horse-shoes that he introduced in the war against the Polaks, and also without knowing how this Ofka Strzegonia comes to be there, although there is a story about her but that took place three hundred years later; she lived in a Silesian convent, later, for decades, then down to an unmarked grave. The man who had a completely different name from Jastrzemb, perhaps Zbylut, went to fight the old Strzegonia, he opened the door, with his sword.

Because someone intervened, one of the Olawans, probably Imko, the mutilated man is saved and taken, unconscious, to his castle. He survives and is present at the coronation of king Przemislaw in 1295 in Gnesen, a silent grey-haired old man with only one arm.

In the door through which he entered Strzegonia's house, the old man plunges two knives. From now on he wears on an iron chain round his neck the misericordia of this Jastrzemb or Zbylut, the short dagger.

We simply say this is

VISION NUMBER FOUR

Very old spirits this time, and very confused ones, who don't know each other's names or families: Strzegonia, Jastrazembiec, Awdaniec, Olawa, Zawora, Starykon, and who confuse the good and bad gods and ghosts: Pomian, Swist Powist, Plon and Plonek and Jescha and Chowaniec. Names, just names. Darkness, a bright day, the shadow swan and the horns. Very old ghosts.

Christina hurries over from the house with a stable lantern and calls out. Grandfather is lying on the seat, slumped on his side. She shakes him and sits him up and as he wakes grandfather says: What is it? and as he stands up, he withdraws his arm from the other hole in the seat, and, so much has he now become a countryman, that he smears the muck over his fingers and regretfully establishes, with regard to its usability: Bit too runny? Sometimes you wonder why these spirits, older and more recent ones, and even some that are very old, why they trouble themselves with him any more: as he has absolutely nothing to say to it all. No there's no joy with such grandfathers. You could argue about it all night long, all through a night that my grandfather passes in perfect peace, as is customary after such emotional upheavals. What is to be done?[1]

[1] Nineteenth sentence.

So to Briesen for the third time. And this time my grandfather must appear in court. So Glinski's purse was filled for
nothing!

So my grandfather regrets the lovely money. If I must go to
Briesen. But why? Utter nonsense.

Nevertheless it turns out to be a lovely trial.

Nebenzahl, we know him. He opens the proceedings and
brings with him.

1. Levin, as accuser.

2. My grandfather, as the accused.

The pair of them sit six feet apart, each one on a brown-
painted bench. Nebenzahl towers above, opposite them. The
whole room is painted brown, that is: the numerous wooden
articles: tables, platform, cupboards, benches, window-frames
and ledges (four), doors (two, one in the side wall, one behind
the judge's table). All painted brown, so as not to show the
fly-dirt, and renovated every year, the benches because of
hard behinds and the cupboards because of hard hands. The
walls too are brown almost half-way to the ceiling.

On the bench behind my grandfather the Reverend Feller and
Brother Rocholl. On the bench behind Levin this girl Marie,
Aunt Huse, old man Habedank. And on the bench behind,
Froese the knacker. Several times during the trial he stands
up and shifts from one side to the other. Nebenzahl has to
warn him to keep still.

Well get on with it, I don't know what it's all about!

Nebenzahl looks at his paper. He says: Complaint. He says
Watermill. He says: Levin. Finally he says: The accused.

He looks at grandfather, who is putting on his best expression. Honourable, peaceable, dignified. A bluish-clouded, milky
layer conceals his black look. He has suspended the watch
chain over his front. Now, as my grandfather sits there, it
stretches slightly over his paunch.

Interrogation of the witnesses.

It materialises immediately that there is no witness present such as District Judge Nebenzahl would wish: one who saw everything, who stood by as the sluice—either that or the pond—was opened.

Wasn't opened, came apart, can happen, this could be the first time. That is the answer my grandfather gives when questioned.

Secretary Bonikowski writes it down.

You tell me your story, says Nebenzahl to Leo Levin. He even says: Herr Levin.

Now Levin must say that my grandfather has always said that something would happen one day. When did the accused make these statements? Was it to you? To whom then?

Aunt Huse gilds the fine proceedings with interruptions, on this occasion: Everyone heard him, anyone will tell you! Who heard him? You?

No, not me.

Be quiet then.

Habedank, commands Aunt Huse, now you speak up!

Herr Habedank? says Judge Nebenzahl. We know each other. My pleasure, says Habedank. And what should he say now? The same as Levin has already said. And the next day, continues Habedank, we stood on the bank with Marie and saw that it never sprang open by itself, Nieswandt agrees. Why have a weir in the first place? There was never one there before.

That's my affair, says my grandfather.

And what exactly was it, Herr Habedank, that made you so sure it didn't spring open by itself?

Nebenzahl is amicable. He listens to Habedank's explanations. But a visit to the scene of the occurrence is a little too much to expect.

He says so and Aunt Huse interrupts immediately: Nonsense, it's all been cleared away ages ago.

So you saw nothing, says Nebenzahl.

Oh but I did.

When, if you please?

Afterwards.

I see, afterwards. Nebenzahl smiles.

That by the way—we haven't mentioned all Aunt Huse's exclamations—was her fourth interruption. This nonsense costs three and a half Talers, an age-old tariff.

Disgraceful, says Aunt Huse, I shan't pay.

Nebenzahl smiles. He could have stepped in at the third interruption, after two warnings. He points this out and, to this fifth interruption, he merely says: My good lady, I didn't hear that.

Aunt Huse rises to her feet. Worthy court, she begins, I must tell you one or two things.

Oh Aunt, sighs Levin.

Be quiet, you can see it's got to be.

So: Worthy court! Here you have a young man, there he is, hard-working, willing, clever, not dear—Levin, look at the Judge—worked with his own hands—Leo, show him your hands!—with these hands he worked, and that's nothing to be ashamed of, built himself this mill, and goes around with the girl that sings like an angel—Marie sing something!

But that's going a little too far, Aunt Huse. Marie's blushing. Habedank says: Go on, Aunt, something else! Although Levin is highly amused to see Marie so shy.

To continue: He goes around with her, as I said, quite respectable, wedding's fixed for next Easter, or it was, and now: What will happen with no mill?

Aunt Huse, as we see, exaggerates a little. Wedding. But there's no harm done here, it's a touching thought.

Yes, says the Aunt, and raises her voice: and there he stands, the scoundrel, this old fellow, so pious and so evil, stands there, muttering away and would probably like to swallow me whole for breakfast. Don't you say anything, I know you, when he was only so high, his pants were always full, you be quiet my lad, what's to become of you, you old *Schadrack*.

Now it gets a little confused. But carry on, Aunt Huse, it doesn't matter. Wonderful woman, says Habedank, and whispers ecstatically three more times: Wonderful woman. I'll tell you something.

Aunt Huse has herself in hand again. She takes a step forwards, raises her fist at the judge's table and cries out in such a shrill, loud voice that Froese leaps up from his seat at the back and remains standing in the gangway between the two rows of benches, his mouth wide open, so that the red-nosed Bonikowski exclaims: Whatever next! and flings his pen into the ink-well:

Must people clear up this Neumühl mess themselves, yes? Without the district court?

Witness! District Judge Nebenzahl has his bell in his hand and is waving it around. Witness Huse, what do you mean by all this. I'll trouble you to respect the dignity of the court. Exactly, replies Aunt Huse briefly and to the point, you might do the same, it would be worth it.

You return to your place, orders Nebenzahl with studied calm. And keep silent. As I see it, your remarks are of no value to this court.

Come on now. Do something. I don't know what all this is about!

So, back and forth and finally: Existing witnesses rejected. Costs? Of course. A new date, after presentation of the witnesses Nieswandt and Korrinth. Poles? And you insist, Herr

Levin? Levin shifts his weight from one foot to the other. He turns round and looks at Aunt Huse.

Well say yes then, shouts Aunt Huse, Levin, I tell you, we'll all come with you.

Yes, says Levin.

A summons will be sent, announces Bonikowski.

But promptly this time, calls Aunt Huse.

Nebenzahl has already closed the case.

Froese, says grandfather, as he goes out, you drove the whole lot of them here.

Just fitted in that way, replies Froese.

Don't let's talk here, says my grandfather.

A town's a town. Briesen is Briesen. All roads lead here, to be precise: to the market place, even more precisely: to Wiezorrek's German House.

A town's a town, mutters Feller absent-mindedly and looks out of the window. These houses, with their tidy front gardens, such a large building, the District President's office, and this strange district court! Green tiles and towers.

It's obvious, a town's a town, there's the women for a start, says Captain von Lojewski, he's there again. Women, I tell you, they're like pebbles on a beach.

Hoho, chortles my grandfather. And turns to the bar: Bring the captain another drink.

Feller giggles a little, he's enjoying the whole affair, perhaps because he emptied his glass in tiny sips. He wags his index finger at the gentleman and tut tuts.

Tell me, Froese, begins my grandfather.

Now Froese is supposed to explain how he comes to be giving a lift to my grandfather's enemies in his German cart.

Froese drinks down the beer that my grandfather bought for him in one gulp, he asks for another beer. I'll pay for it myself, he says and straightway fumbles the money out of his lower right jacket pocket and likewise downs this glass at a single gulp and says, in my grandfather's direction, whilst his left little finger pokes the corner of his eye: I'll whisper something in your ear.

That sounds rather impertinent. Lojewski leans back. This is hardly suitable company for an officer. What are these people, knackers? Froese the knacker stands up, he says to Feller who is also about to rise: You just stay sitting down, and to my grandfather he says: You are a first class criminal.

With this, the twentieth of our sentences, Froese leaves the German House.

And picks up his guests from Uncle Sally's. They're just coming out.

First Aunt Glickle, but she's not coming. With cheerful chatter: My little ones, and: I've packed rolls for you.

And a bottle of coffee, says Habedank and hands Froese the bottle wrapped in an old felt cloth.

Now they clamber in. Aunt Huse first. Habedank and Levin have to lend a helping hand. Marie jumps up, then Levin, finally Habedank, next to Froese on the driving-seat.

Then off they go, calling down and back, and Uncle Sally runs beside them for a while. And they're not very far out of the town, before Falkenau and before the railway-crossing, when Aunt Huse begins to sing. Because it's late afternoon.

> How sweet the peal
> O'er wood and field.
> Of the bugle's lilting song.

That's a real song! A long pause after every line and the naturally sustained Peal and Field.

> With it's echo long, so long.

Marie's gypsy alto. And Aunt Huse's sharp soprano. Habe-dank has a tenor like an old oboe, although sometimes he pops in little clarinet-trills. Then Levin laughs and Froese counters with a deep, dark tuba-note, practically a roar. Sometimes, from the nearby pastures, a cow answers back. Then Marie can't go on. And then, for a moment, only Aunt Huse's soprano lilts in the mild, dusty summer air, which smells of new-mown hay and is stirred only by the voices or a horse-brake or the little black flies which settle round the animals' eyes and rise up in a swarm when the horses toss their heads.

And so they come to Polkau.

In Polkau it's dark already.

As dark as it can be in a clear night.

Get up, by night, and go to the window.

In the distance is the sound of running water, a stream, you hear it now: this scarcely audible, rhythmic pulse of calm water flowing interrupted only by the nocturnal hunting fish and, further down river, just before the little stream meets the Drewenz, the hurrying otter. And the sharp sound as they thrust their heads out of the water.

The fish has snapped a fly and the otter snorts once in the night air.

It must seem to anyone here that never can the world have been so still before. The second crop of grass is tougher in the blade, it bends unwillingly at the touch of the ground-wind and rights itself as soon as the force subsides. A rippling sound. Only the crickets are loud, but their voices are part of the stillness and simply cause it to vibrate a little.

Even the footsteps coming through the grass are part of it. Slow footsteps. Faltering. And now, words.

Where was I for so long?

You are at the window. You see her walking, a tiny figure:

Josepha. You can't call: Josepha! She won't hear you. Too far away.

Where was I for so long?

In a foreign land, Josepha, I know. But what do you want by the water's edge? Go back, you are drunk.

Where was I for so long?

In a foreign land, Josepha. Only when you were drunk did it seem otherwise. That was just an illusion.

You watch, she goes towards the water, hesitant, she tosses back her head, stands with her hands on her breast. Her face alight.

Cry out, she won't hear you.

Step back from the window, do as you're told now.

Josepha went on. In to the sluggish water. In to this stream that carries her away.

CHAPTER TWELVE

The gust of wind had passed now. On the ground lay a stricken moth moving its wing.

We are telling a story here. A fact that is easily forgotten. We have introduced twenty sentences, there are fourteen more to come.

Habedank kept to the field-track. The gust of wind, which had descended like a stone over a steep cliff, directly in front of him, now took off over the fields, splintered now into six or seven differently pitched air-currents, describing curves and loops at different heights, suffering little set-backs, sometimes just stumbling along.

So it was, a couple of days before the journey in Froese's cart. This journey to Briesen.

Habedank stood on the field track which runs from the north, from the mountain-range behind the Struga, to the little wood between Gronowo and Trzianek and out of the wood came another man. He wore a long coat, in summer, and a black hat. That's how they met: Habedank, the gypsy violinist and Geethe, Johann Vladimir, the village flutist, formerly from Bohemia and now Hoheneck, but not for much longer.

They greet according to the circumstances of their acquaintance, which is, as colleagues. *Do stu piorunow!*

Geethe the flutist turned round and accompanied Habedank back to Jan Marcin, where he had been and where Habedank was heading for. And then they sat behind the house on the chopped fire-wood and Geethe whistled: When I ask the wanderer, where have you been. In clink, Habedank had replied. Not direct, but fairly. *Do stu piorunow!*

What makes them like that, says Geethe the flutist. He means these German authorities and this German grandfather and this German policeman that disappeared. But how should Habedank reply?

None of them's a musician.

Geethe the flutist continues. Someone must.

Habedank the violinist hasn't said a word.

But what Geethe doesn't know, is that the District President can play the piano very nicely, and Nebenzahl too. But does that make them musicians?

No, no Geethe, not one of them's a musician.

If all four of them were sitting together, here, Weiszmantel, Habedank, Geethe, Willuhn, and they could determine future events in Neumühl, in Malken, in Briesen—how quickly we would get on with our story, and settle the whole question.

During this conversation on the wood-pile behind Jan Marcin's house, Habedank had deliberated for a while before suddenly interrupting Geethe's spirited coda—he had resumed his concert with a waltz fantasia: Pious folk, these Germans. At this, Vladimir Geethe set down his instrument, and, with a serious face and booming voice, cried Haha! that's all, and then his final cadence.

And, when he was finished, Habedank had said: It's not because of being pious, Aunt Huse, you know, she's pious. And it's not because of being German. Aunt Huse is German, you know.

And now Geethe the flutist perceived that a lack of music is also not the explanation.

Well the simple answer, concluded Geethe, is that it's all because of money.

Could be. My grandfather has money. The company at Briesen too.

And Krolikowski? No, not him. And Feller not much either. Not even Glinski, although he has more.

It's quite simple, Geethe had declared, the one lot because they have some and want to hang on to it and the others because they want it and get paid for running errands. You're bound to be right. With that Habedank had stood up. I'm going in now. Tomorrow we're going to Briesen with Levin, Froese the knacker, is taking us. Trial date, you know. And he left the next day. And now he's back.

The air is still scented with jasmine, from the countless bushes stretching from the wood to the Chaussee, and sweeping down from the Chaussee, though less densely now, through the meadows to Neumühl, and from there down to the mill stream, a chain of green and white.

How long the hawthorn and black alder blossomed this year. And the lilac. Everything is blossoming longer this year than before.

Blossom's always like that when there's sorrow abroad, says Habedank.

But what sad talk this is. Jan Marcin is walking around indoors clapping his hands, he grabs the broom and dances round the chairs and finally, puffed out, sits on the table and yells at the top of his voice.

Just listen, Marie cries, and now they stop talking, all of them, sitting there: Habedank and Geethe, Weiszmantel, Willuhn, Antonja and Scarletto and Leo Levin.

Music, yells Jan Marcin.

That won't be difficult. Willuhn has had his box on his knees the whole time. It has acquired a new patch, from an old leather cloth which was already perished, but it will do for a while. Now the box is almost whole.

There he sits and plays, two fourths, with a short introduction, left left right left right left right, just as your legs move of their own accord.

Do you remember, Geethe says quietly, ten years ago, do you remember.

And Habedank remembers it well, they all do, the Poles and the Germans, it's a little more than ten years ago, eleven in fact, it left its mark on all of them: They came to life in Congress-Poland, in the duchy of Posen, in Galicia where the Tzar's soldiers were camped, and the Prussians and the Austrians. Do you remember, shouts Weiszmantel, and he can't sit still any longer, and Habedank remembers: Those men with the scythes.

The thought of it makes Weiszmantel sing, to Willuhn's melody.

Jan Marcin stands there and has no more need of his broom, and Antonja puts her hands on her hips and Antonio and Antonella come inside and stand in the doorway, Weiszmantel sings:

> The time had come, this time I cried,
> My soul was sore oppressed.
> O how I cried, O, far and wide,
> This was not at my behest.
>
> Emperor says and King says, voice so cold,
> Uproot this Polish weed,
> From this soul both hard and old,
> Village, town and court shall be freed.
>
> On horseback rides the Tzar's own knight,
> Many knights to kill us all,

Who shall say what is wrong and right,
For Starost and priests there is no call.

But scythes, scythes, scythes, sunk deep
In helve, and in hands,
And foes will come on horses sleek
To bring an end to these our lands.

At evening man and moon see
Riders, riders, filled with hate,
And then we left. For where we
Lived is smoke. O brother can you weep our fate?

Yes, how do we feel? Here come the tears that we had forgotten to weep. Jan Marcin's tears and Geethe's and Marie's
tears. Levin's tears, and what shall we say now?

Willuhn, the drinker, sinks his grey head into his hands, and
Jan Marcin, who has never touched a drop, gulps and sucks
in air between his teeth, like a drowning man.

We'll say: 1863, in January, the Poles left their houses and
left their villages, in the duchy of Posen, in Galicia, in the
kingdom of Warsaw or the kingdom of Poland or Congress-
Poland, which is the same thing, and stood in the fields in a
winter which was not very severe, but still winter enough,
in seven hundred skirmishes and in the battle of the scythes
and the Great Russians and White Russians with them, and
the Ukrainians, Hungarians, Czechs and Germans, French
and Italians—many or just a few, but that's immaterial, the
Polish sons and the Polish fathers took up their scythes and
brandished them against the cavalry which the Margrave,
the Warsaw governor, the cur Wielopolski had set loose on
them, to infest the land. Everywhere, that year, the farmers
came out to face them, in front of their villages and their

forests, and, in the towns, the other Poles came out into the streets leading to the squares, where the cry for Polish freedom rang out.

The end was in Weiszmantel's song: Where we lived, is smoke. Tears. But tears of anger. And above the anger soars pride. Pride which has survived the ten or eleven years since then, living pride.

Weiszmantel is silent. He stands there, white-haired, like Jan Marcin beside him. Willuhn tinkers on with his tune, left right left right, one two one two, softer now and a little slower. Where are we?

In the fields of Russia-Poland, in Cracow, in Kielce, in a wood to the south of the Lysa Gord. Anywhere, but always there, where they will not rest content.

So the evening has come. There is still light at the windows. Evening is beautiful.

In front of the house stands Scarletto's Italian Circus, with horse and cart and all the animals. They will come and see to you for the night: you, Emilio, you Francesca, you, Casimiro and Tosca you too of course. Come Antonio, let those that will, talk, you know what has to be done.

Now night is creeping in. There are no mountains here from which she could stride down to the music of darkness and so she slowly covers the plain, from across the meadows, from the Struga and up from the Drewenz and perhaps from as far back as the reed-ponds by Garczewo. In her wake is the croaking of frogs and the endless, indefinable chirping of crickets.

In Jan Marcin's house it's dark. Just voices now, there's Weiszmantel talking, and Antonja whispering to the children, who can't get straight to sleep because it's Sunday tomorrow. Like tiny sparks the sounds flit through the darkness over the table and up to the ceiling. Jan Marcin's black cat draws himself up as though to snatch at them, but he only stretches out one paw and then withdraws it. He's not asleep. His green slit eyes follow the voices and movements which gradually die away. Finally he is alone with Jan Marcin who lays his old hand on the cat's head. *Kotek*, he says and : *Poznojuz*. It's getting late, little tom-cat. And there the pair of them sit. Tomorrow we'll be on our own again, says Jan Marcin. Night has reached the Chaussee, now it's over Gronowo, past Neumühl, heading for Gollub, down the Drewenz and then, who knows where? Cool air hovers over the wide valley bearing the Vistula and its pulsing silence.

Jan Marcin strokes the cat. And the cat rolls over on its side and stretches out its legs. And so the daylight comes. This Sunday dawns in shades of grey. And no rain shall spoil it for us.

CHAPTER THIRTEEN

Whether or not day breaks, depends on the hens.

Jan Marcin's Italian hen stands in front of Francesca's cage, trumpeting her dawn-cry over and over again to the tree-tops. But Francesca merely lifts her head with its ruffled comb, opens one eye, blinks and shuts it again. What are you making such a noise for, little Goldilocks?

Now, in the morning stillness, you can hear the far-off hens of Trzianek, young ones and old ones, and, when the wind changes, those from Gronowo and Neuhof. And the Gronowo hens hear the Neumühl ones and call back. And now day struggles to its feet over the meadows, first to its knees, then, with a shiver of its coat, and a wild jerk, on to its legs, to stretch and toss back its head with a snort.

In the middle of his bedroom, in his nightshirt, stands Alwin Feller. With the deepest sentiments of loneliness.

This we must freely admit. He regrets the passing of his wife, this close companion of fears and quarrels, who never ceased to be a stranger. Why, Feller keeps asking, why? When he has posed the question for long enough, anger wells up inside him. To be sure, it was obvious at the burial, that the brothers and sisters sympathised with him in this whole sorry business, which makes it simpler, but not easier.

What could have got in to her? She was wandering about the house again. Christina had brought her back and talked to her, and even came again the following day. To talk again. But no, not a word, just wandered about and stood still, her face—as white as chalk.

Could it have been that blow with the book? But that wasn't the first in her life, not even the first in this marriage. The whole affair is a mystery to Feller. Well, it is quite difficult to comprehend how one person could die from another's meanness. Wanders around, says nothing and suddenly gone. It's a complete mystery to you Feller and it just makes you angry. Didn't she have everything here? And then again, still more righteous: Anger.

Aren't you going to say your morning-prayer, Alwin Feller, preacher, shepherd of your congregation? Shall the blackbird and the lark put you to shame, as it says in the song?

No, he does not say his morning-prayer, he says: The word which goeth forth from my mouth, shall not return empty. Thus sayeth the Lord.

Those are his words, it sounds a bit stale to us, and he kneels in the middle of the room in his nightshirt.

In my grandfather's house there are not many mansions, indeed not, but a host of people. All pious and all German, we establish, although pious and German are necessarily not the same. Sometimes they coincide. In the case of Aunt Huse, as Habedank said. In some other cases too, we would add and we'll elevate this comment to the status of a twenty-first sentence and we'll include the twenty-second at the same time: There are people and people.

One kind congregate around my grandfather. Perhaps Christina alone is one of the other kind. Or brother Gustav and his wife too, these Malken Evangelists who sprinkle their children. Perhaps they belong to the other kind too. And Olga Wendehold, the Adventist. These are namely also present. The two kinds mingle somewhat here at the Baptists' summer-fair, which, God preserve us, is not to enlarge the Malken Union. No, indeed not.

Christina is racing about the house, in to the kitchen, out to the yard, to the empty carriages, it's a lovely day. She was so happy that she put on her blackest dress, the plain black one, the one reserved for important occasions, the really expensive one, which keeps its silky sheen a whole lifetime and is always the best one, this really lovely dress. With a black open-work scarf to match. And black shoes and black stockings. Everything else snow white. And the house is full already, all pious souls as we said. Pusch and Kuch and Puschke and Kuchel and Puschinski and Kucharski, the Elders of the communities of Gollub and Linde. All with wives and grown-up children, and the relatives from Malken and father-in-law Fagin from Little Brudzaw and Christina's brother Heinrich from Lissewo with his wife Emilie Amalie. The old ones sitting and the young ones standing. Jemiljejemalje, calls mother Puschke from the sofa, do go and see Christina about the coffee.

Just coming, Aunt Wife gently assures her, just coming. The cups are there, and the cakes.

Oh dear, the cream is in the kitchen.

Mother Puschke and sister Kucharski are chattering nineteen to the dozen. Hay and potato lifting and wind and weather. I think we're in for a storm, says mother Puschke. But that thundering noise is no thunder, but rather, as we know, my grandfather's ram behind the barn, who is excited and charging against the beams, the so-called Mahlke, so called because he was bought from Mahlke the dealer. And sister Kucharski answers: Hmm. And says: Last year we had a little drop in the corner, with Josepha. And sighs.

Then Kucharski says: Be still, you silly old goat.

Now listen here, Kucharski!

But, as we said, coffee. And griddle scones. And poppy-cakes. Grandfather comes in, wearing a tie. Well here we are, he says.

And now Feller arrives and is given coffee and then they all go out of grandfather's house, linger for a while in the court-yard and at the gate and, then make their way, dressed in black carrying hymn-books, on both sides of the sandy cart-track to the chapel and go inside, Feller leading the way, and kneel down between the benches, resting their heads on the wooden rail in front, Voice of Faith on the right, close by, and awkwardly they rise to their feet again, Kuch as usual knocking his knee, although the foot-rests and floor-boards are scoured, and finally they take their seats. And now the Reverend Feller steps up to the desk and says: Brothers and Sisters, beloved in the Lord.

Now the summer-festival of the Baptist community in Neumühl is under way. Feller begins: O Soul, come flying to the cross.

It begins for one voice and lilts along gently, interrupted twice as grandfather clears his throat, but then:

O come, come to the cross,
To the cross now make your way!

For four voices now. And where the women have to hang on to the notes, on the last syllable of each line, tenor and bass repeat: Come to the cross! and: Make your way!

And Christ, the Lord, will give,
Will give you his peace today.

On the first 'will give' the soprano has a very pretty slurred note: first down a third and then up a fifth, whilst the other voices continue the melody until a sudden pause for every-one: after the second 'will give'. Then, his peace today quiet and quieter, sustained by soprano and bass, above and below the organist, flourishes of the middle voices, till it dies away.

Perhaps it's not familiar to everyone, but it's still very good. To be sure, my grandfather has other worries, but we're not talking about them now. What's the point of a summer festival, he broods, and has his reasons, harvest festival's enough but we're not going into that either. It's the summer fair, and that's that.

What's Fellers' theme for today?

There he stands, black, arms stretched out to the side, voice loud and slow. At the last word in every sentence his mouth snaps shut with such an air of finality, that the ends of his mongol moustaches continue to quiver for a second or two. It's impossible to tell whether or not he has finished. But no Amen, with long e, so there's more to come. And here the eagle of faith, the dove of gentleness, the pelican of self-sacrificing love and other feathered friends, nourished by our Heavenly Father take wing together under the roof towards the shining window behind the desk. Rocholl stands up and walks past Feller to the window and opens it wide and Feller turns to him as he walks back and says: Let in the sunshine.

And that is the song they've all been waiting for.

Christina begins immediately and too high, but it can never be high enough for her voice.

Rocholl first returns to his place, then, still standing, joins in and sits down singing. His aunt nudges him in the ribs and nods at him, mouth full of the song and suddenly stops singing and bends over him to say: Alwin, Heavens above, doesn't he look dreadful.

True enough.

Then they all stand up and say together: . . . discover, heart of mine, discover the ways of my eyes and mind, tell me if the evil path I tread—

Here my grandfather breaks off and lets the others continue. He looks across at Feller, but Feller is staring into space as though paralysed, hair awry, tears streaming down his face. My grandfather starts in alarm and only recovers himself in time to catch the last words: along the eternal path.

All around him, everywhere, left and right and behind him, the weeping has begun, a whole rain-shower, interspersed with the rustling of black silk dresses as handkerchiefs are brought out, then noses being blown and mens' attempts to comfort: Yes I know, it's all right. And grandfather to Christina: Wipe your nose.

As though it were the funeral all over again.

Through the open windows, bursting with light, you see the churchyard, and Josepha's grave. Lying under blackish-green wreaths and white flowers. See the bright wooden cross, hung with a thin wreath of white clover. Weiszmantel's wreath.

Women, my grandfather would dearly love to say, should never be allowed inside chapel.

He refrains from saying it. He sits down noisily and opens his Voice of Faith for the next hymn: Humbly I gaze in wonder. Yes, is anyone here going to carry on with the singing?

At any rate, in Rosinke's tavern concertina, violin and flute are being played, now, on a Sunday morning, in the middle of a pious village.

Rosinke strolls in, fat, in shirt and trousers, on a Sunday morning and stands in front of the bar.

It's no use today, my door's staying shut, the New Fellow is racing about poking his nose in everywhere.

He means constable Adam, who is not racing anywhere at the moment but still sitting in the chapel, you must be seen everywhere. Just like a puppy-dog running around, comments Frau Rosinke and: You must go now.

They go out through the back door, Geethe, Willuhn, Weiszmantel, Habedank and Marie and Antonella, these two are inseparable. But then Rosine says: Music in the morning, because it sounds nice after all. Sit down behind the barn, if you like, and you can have a few bottles.

They sit behind the barn, in a circle round Weiszmantel, who is just about to embark on a story about the hero Stephan.

Was such a young fellow, says Weiszmantel, only twenty years old and jet-black hair, a red and white lad, a blood and milk lad. Studied himself some learning. And suddenly, just after the Christmas of '62 he stands at his brother's door in Warsaw, stands at the door and says: It's all starting, next week. What's got in to you, the brother says, the Margrave—that's this Wielopolski—he'll show you. Go back and learn in your school.

But the lad replies: You're a fine Pole, turns and goes, a fortnight, three weeks later it's all starting. Hei hei hei hei! And young Stephan, the eaglet, always at the front, has a fine voice and cries out good and loud: Down with Herr Margrave, and the Kossacks too.

You did some fine hacking down, give it him, and again, murmurs Willuhn dreamily. Sing the one about the scythes.

> The time had come, the time I cried
> My soul was sore oppressed.

This is no summer festival. Weiszmantel's shrill old voice trembles and breaks on the highest note: Soul. Then the melody climbs back from deep down the scale: Sore oppressed. Weiszmantel holds his violin horizontally, resting on his chest and evenly strokes the same three notes over and over again, at equal intervals, after every line Willuhn plays two bars of intermezzo, full of chords, and above Weiszmantel's tenor, now almost like the voice of a young boy, Vladimir Geethe's flute hovers with thin whistles and unexpected flat trills and suddenly descends with a counterpart to the vicinity of Weiszmantel's melody.

O how I cried, O, far and wide.

They sing: Marie, Antonella. Willuhn always coming in on the last line.

Nieswandt comes striding through the potato field and calls across to them from some way away: Well, how's the summer-fair? Don't mention summer-fair. Just music. But that rings out as far as Germann's courtyard, where Korrinth is sitting saying Hoho to Levin, who just replies: We'll see.

It rings out, seven verses long, only the words are not clear. What's Weiszmantel singing now, we surely don't know this verse?

I go, we all go, come with me,
Over water and mountain sheer,
One says to the other: You will see
Eagles fly, red eagles here.

But Weiszmantel, that's not right: red or black eagles, the red one comes from the south and under its wings the Vistula waters swirl, and out of the northern spheres, the black one hovers in the sky with outstretched claws—it's not right. There are people and people—that was our twenty-second sentence. Now we'll gather the second kind around us. The first kind are enjoying their summer fair.

Constable Adam puts in another appearance in front of the chapel door. With his cap, or helmet, as it's called. Official expression, garnished with a touch of summer festivity. Then: right hand to head-gear and off.

He comes round the corner of the barn, stops and says: Singing and playing of musical instruments after previous announcement only.

Come a little closer, says Habedank.

I'll give you come closer, the deceased Krolikowski would have replied, Adam is a little more refined, he takes three steps forward. Very sorry, he says, Regulations.

And there stands Korrinth, who has followed Adam, stands there and starts talking and refuses to be interrupted. What d'you mean: Regulations?

Here he comes from the pious chapel and has just sung: Be of good cheer, good cheer, the sun shines every day, comes pissing up here, with cold nose and eyes like shit, just mind you don't do it in your pants.

Spit.

The Adam thus addressed waves the words aside. Silence, and duty is duty.

Let's go to Germann's place, suggests Korrinth.

If you wish, says Adam. Three fingers to head-gear. Turns and goes, in to Rosinke's. And once inside: Herr Rosinke. You know the regulations. No service today.

But why ever shouldn't I know them, Officer, I know everything. Adam casts a brief sidelong glance at the bottle standing ready.

Maybe you fancy a little something, interposes Rosinke's wife attentively, just a drop.

Not at the moment. I'm on duty.

Then you'll take a bottle with you, yes?

The little bottle just fits snugly in Adam's breast pocket.

Smart fellow, comments Frau Rosinke, when the constable has gone.

We've got him where we want him, says Rosinke. Let's fetch up some more.

There are, as we said, people and people, but Schnapps is always the same, that's the way Rosinke looks at it.

With Nieswandt and Willuhn in the lead, they make their

way through the village. Weiszmantel, Marie and Antonella, Geethe with Korrinth, last of all Habedank. A welcoming in Germann's courtyard.

My grandfather is just sitting down to his mid-day meal with Feller beside him, and is lucky enough not to see the turmoil, but if he made an effort, he could hear it at least. But with him are his other worries, the ones that troubled him in chapel this morning. What's the point of this summer festival? It doesn't suit my grandfather at all, not one little bit. And those, admittedly, are dark, foreboding words. But dark words are dark words. Sometimes we see as through a glass darkly, and again sometimes we don't. In the case of these dark words at any rate, we do not.

Now they have reached the courtyard of Gregor Germann Owner of thirty-six acres of fields and meadows, maids and man-servants and cattle. A Catholic Pole, like his neighbour Lebrecht. Housing, for the present, my grandfather's dismissed mill-workers, Korrinth and Nieswandt. Everything in the yard now, round the well, where the grass grows tall: music and Poles and gypsies and Willuhn with his bottle and Leo Levin on an old brick. And now the circus-people are arriving, through Lebrecht's garden which has a gate to Germann's yard. With as much gaiety as sunshine and as much noise as gaiety.

Then Germann goes in to the house and says to his wife, in Polish: This is getting a bit much, you know, this hoard of rabble in my yard, you know. And Germann's wife tilts her nose in the air, which is not easy as the flat lump protrudes only slightly from the wide expanse of flat face, and says: Down and outs. And when they begin to sing outside, because it's impossible to do otherwise: in this weather and amongst so many well-disposed friends and acquaintances, and that song is there, the one which makes your ears hum, all night long, after you have heard it once: Poland is not lost yet—proclaimed by all the instruments, and when Weisz-mantel springs to his feet outside, and here in the house the woman grabs her shawl, flings it round her, joins in singing and makes for the door, at the sound of this song Germann says: I don't want any trouble, it's my yard. And runs out, past his wife.

And stands in the yard, facing the pack of good-for-nothings: the two children, leaning on the right and left of Antonja, this shining flame from the darkness, Habedank, more speaking than singing each word across his violin, Weiszmantel who has leant back his white head and is calling up to heaven, hands outstretched, this lovely Marie, Scarletto, who has raised his hat. What was it that Germann wanted to say?

And he says nothing. He walks round the crowd, stops here and there, and then the song is over. Now he says: The old *czart* sings like a bullfrog, and points to Weiszmantel and says: Go to the devil. The words, meant to sound commanding, came out, if anything rather pleasantly. But after all he has found a sensible one amongst them, this Habedank.

And so he says: Gypsy, you know, there'll be trouble. Go somewhere else, not just now, not straight away, by and by will do. Slowly. Gregor, we must admit, has had a little bit too much, lands and cattle and not all goods, though maybe yes; marriage is no horse-deal, they say and: Whoever doesn't marry money marries nothing—but he did marry money, ten years ago now, he came from Kielce then with nothing at all. Don't you touch any of that, thinks Germann. And thinks: It plods on nicely all the while, without any fuss, keep the peace here and keep the peace there. Peace.

Habedank knows this Germann, he knows just what sort of a fellow he is. Children, says Habedank, my stomach's hanging down to my knee-caps, and takes Marie with him, and Weiszmantel and Willuhn.

Summer-fair, where's this summer-fair, asks Geethe the flutist, he's going to embellish it, he calls after Willuhn: To the summer-fair.

And Willuhn shouts back and waves the bottle. Give it him. In Briesen it's quite different, says my grandfather, if only you had seen: the summer-fair in Briesen.

And Tomaschowski says: Where isn't it different.

And Kaminski: Here under the alders.

There they sit in the alder-wood, by the mill-stream, a little further up than the mill, on the swiftly assembled benches, on un-planed planks, and lying all around, on horse-blankets, the other Baptist menfolk, and the Baptist children are flinging cow-pats in to the river for the fish, no stones of course, as they would chase the fish away. And the Baptist women-folk are sitting in two large groups, the younger ones in the sun, congregated around Alwin Feller who is dressed all in black high up to the neck, and they are talking about all the beauty in the world, and the older ones round a tree, in the shade, and their conversations are concerned with other things, with the cross and sorrow, in other words sundry sufferings: rheumatics, ganglions, St. Anthony's fire, weak chests and, at this very moment, varicose veins.

That's the way it is. From the beginning, you think it'll pass, but no, just look at yourself, doesn't go, not a chance. In Briesen it's quite different, declares my grandfather and struggles to his feet and looks around: Even a trumpet chorus!

So what, says Fenske, those little whistles. Haven't we got fine music?

What do you know about it, says my grandfather, it might be good enough for Sadlinken.

When the dogs join in, adds Kossakowski disdainfully.

You lot, always pretending you're such fine folk, says Fenske.

It's good! Listen!

But who will listen? Not the women, they have plenty to talk about, open mouths mean ears closed, and so the chatter is always lively, each one must relate what the other already knows. And the men have their conversational topics: Dreadful these days, they're even starting to demand their rights. Yes, the good old days, says Kossakowski. To Michaelis, when they left: one Taler, that was enough, not a penny more. They mean the Polish labourers.

Golden days, they were, says my grandfather, and it's all to do with the fear of God, which is on the decline, you see.

No they are not listening. Though Geethe is conjuring up a whole bohemian fair, songs to dance to and dances to sing to, airy tents with pointed roofs and coloured bunting, roundabouts with horses, swings. But no, who's going to listen?

Well coffee then, here in the open, plum tarts. Well, little musicians, says Christina, help yourselves.

A speech before the coffee and a lovely song, Christina's song: Heart, my heart, when will you be free.

With which she still can't sing away her sorrow, Christina is spared nothing, there's no other way.

And the same old jokes: Adam had seven sons.

Enough to make you do it in your pants, says old Frau Kuch, with a face as long as a poker.

Finally Barkowski with his lovely song:

> When the lightning cracks and the thunder claps
> And everything's wet from the rain.

And he doesn't just sing, he grabs my grandfather around the hips and dances off with him, yelling at the top of his voice.

Then it's so lovely to be on the Alps.

Now, old Frau Kuch says to Christina: Such pious folk prancing about, enough to make you do it in your pants.
Always Brother Barkowski, at every summer fair: last of all this song.
And then, in large and small groups, back to the village. The women singing, all but the really old ones who are threatening: We'll have to have a look at those little bottoms.
Because the children don't want to go to bed yet.
What's all this about no service, says Rosinke; he can just try coming over here.
But Adam does not come. At any rate not immediately.
But others come instead.
Barkowski is standing in the doorway waving his arms and he calls back down the stairs: Surely we're not amongst pledgers.
God forbid, Kucharski mutters darkly from outside.
Leading up to Rosinke's shop-door is a bricked staircase. Five steps. And a wooden banister-rail on which this dark spokesman from Gollub is hauling himself up.
He says, No, pledgers never, Heavens above!
In Gollub, you see, there are these Pledgers who don't drink, not even on high days and holidays, particularly not on high days and holidays. Heavens above!
Don't imagine there's only Barkowski and Kucharski and no one else. They are all following up, Pusch and Puschinski, the folk from Linde and Gollub and Kuchel Kuch and Puschke and Kuchel and my grandfather with brother Gustav and brothers-in-law Henry and father Fagin, Rocholl, Tomas-

chowski, Kossakowski, about whom we weren't going to say any more, and Kaminski. And Fenske from Sadlinken too. Still later Feller arrives. The last to come, as we shall see, is constable Adam. Yet Feller took his time.

Yet they are not the last, Feller and Adam. But the first, Barkowski and Kucharski, weren't really the first either. In the bar-parlour, by the open window were already seated gypsies and cottagers and tramps and Willuhn. And Geethe was piping away to a horrible ballad that Weiszmantel was performing with many Ta ta tas and La la las and interruptions because such songs sometimes get too gruesome: About the great Herr Wishowat: who is hanging from a stake, head downwards and the Czar Basilowitsch with a huge stick in his hand, screaming as if his tongue were ripped out. Now the Boyars step forward and they've understood what he wants, and each one has a sword. One hacks off an ear, the next one the other ear, one the nose, one cuts off his lips, no one takes his hair, that's dripping with blood.

God, O God, on Sunday! says Rosinke's wife, leaning over the bench, perhaps to understand the Lalas and Tatas and probably to put the correct interpretation on Weiszmantel's silences.

More!

Now the Boyar who cuts off his sex.

And now the Czar rushes in, red-eyed, flings his royal hat on the ground, stamps the earth and rattles through his foam-filled mouth: Cur, eat it. And holds his royal sword inlaid with rubies against this Boyar, who is an average fellow of fairly calm passions and stands there, wondering, will the same happen to him if he doesn't obey?

To Geethe's piping flute.

I must say! Willuhn stretches a little and scratches between

194

his shoulder blades, sitting on the bench. That's the way history looks! And we remember: Willuhn is a school master, albeit sacked, but he can't get it out of his blood. Fortunately he's quite nice in other respects. And it goes without saying that Weiszmantel is too.

And then the Baptists came, and so: Roses bloom on the moorland grave. Something melancholy. And afterwards:

> Watch how Opalinski creeps
> Been in mud seven weeks.

In other words something German.

As though that were any good.

What are you doing here, says Rocholl.

My grandfather puts it a different way, he says: Rosinke, what's this, I thought it was closed company?

Well, says Rosinke, there's room enough, you could sit over there, I thought.

So Rosinke thinks too, in his capacity as inn-keeper.

Don't talk such rubbish to me, says my grandfather and shoves back father-in-law Fagin, who was just saying: Playing fine music, these gypsies.

At this moment Feller comes in the door and sees straight away what's happening, and runs up to Willuhn. Herr Willuhn, he says, we are celebrating our annual summer-fair here. In the ale-house, asks Willuhn. Better and better.

Willuhn has the wrong idea. Because the Protestants in Malken don't have summer-fairs.

Herr Willuhn, Feller repeats emphatically.

But here Frau Rosinke interrupts: What do you mean by ale-house, Herr Willuhn. We are a respectable tavern.

Indeed it's there outside for all to read, inscribed over the door: Tavern and Hotel. Proprietor Hermann Rosinke. And underneath, in smaller letters: First house facing the square.

Well then, are we going to sit over there, asks Fenske and makes his way to the corner by the stove.

But grandfather cannot only see this Willuhn and this flutist from Hoheneck, but the tramps and gypsies as well and there too are Nieswandt and Korrinth, his—admittedly one-time workers. So grandfather, after a proud glance sweeping the assembled company, declares: I'm not sitting down with Poles.

Those are grandfather words, and we'll count them, although they are not all that new: Number twenty-three.

To which Geethe the flutist replies. He says: You could behave yourself a bit better, I should have thought, more like a decent human being, what's your name?

Grandfather is stunned for a moment. That's the limit!

But Feller is already standing in front of him, saying: Johann, leave it to me, and starting on again about summer-fairs and soon he's on the peace of the Sabbath, which must be to the pious spirit as the cornfield in the glow of evening. Cast a glance outside, my friends. You are seated by the window. That's where we are and that's where we're staying, says Willuhn, ex-teacher.

Oh, stay there, Fenske mutter irritably. Perhaps we'll get something to drink in a minute. He has obviously missed the point entirely.

Herr Fenske, says Habedank and stands up. But now Rosinke elbows his way to the front of the stage, it could be getting serious here. He stands between my grandfather and this Feller and these musicians and Poles and says: No quarrelling, please. And as Adam is just this minute entering the room, he says, and says it bluntly and firmly in order to forestall every possible intention of Adam's: Constable, would you come here a moment. Adam raises two fingers to his helmet: Herr Rosinke, what's the matter then?

We don't need policemen here, go home again, says Rocholl and attempts to follow Fenske's example and sit by the stove. So it's come to this, says my grandfather bitterly, you can't sit yourself down in peace anywhere.

Do the gypsies upset you, Fagin calls over to brother Gustav, from beside the stove, have they been playing all afternoon? Silence, commands my grandfather. Either them or us, Herr Rosinke!

Not even all the Baptists quite understand, not even all the Neumühlers. And certainly not the guests.

Well, clear off then, says Korrinth and shakes Willuhn by the arm. Come on, let's have a tune!

Silence, commands my grandfather, but no one hears, Willuhn has started to play. Old Friends. Habedank comes straight in with a double-stopping, which sounds like a treble-double, Geethe trills masterfully above them.

And to the sound of this fine marching music the Germans from Neumühl, Linde and Gollub come over beside the stove. Just my grandfather requires a gentle shove from constable Adam who, in doing so, puts a hand on his shoulders until grandfather brushes it off. Kindly keep your greasy fingers to yourself, constable, I'll trouble you to remember that in future.

I suspected this fellow from the start, thinks grandfather as he slowly walks over to the stove. Someone with a name like that. He won't grow old here.

Does he perhaps assume he will grow old here? That is the twenty-fourth sentence. And now Schnapps.

Rosine is kept busy. First to one side, then the other. Innkeeper Rosinke would like to stay behind his bar, but his wife can't manage, so he goes over with the bottle, but now he must be careful not to chalk up too few on the slate.

The ladies are coming along, aren't they, asks Rosine.

Of course, says Kucharski.

They're coming to fetch us, laughs Fagin, but we're not going. Get the lemonades ready, says Rosine to her husband. But it never comes to that. Firstly the ladies are busy talking, at Rocholl's, where the aunt is still a guest, at Christina's, where the last tears are wept for Josepha, and goodness knows where else. And secondly this gypsy music is getting on grandfather's nerves.

It obviously affects him differently from Fenske, who has already struck up a conversation diagonally across the bar-parlour, and differently from Puschinski and Kuchel who are knocking back glass after glass to make up for this dry, dry day and the dreary sing-song, and differently from brother-in-law Heinrich from Lissewo, who is already in the lead, sitting there raising his glass to the musicians and calling: Landlord, a round for the gentlemen.

Here he means the gypsies and so forth, at which grandfather can only growl. And suddenly scream, in Rosinke's direction: But not for Polacks!

Then not for me either, says Geethe.

Brother-in-law Heinrich is still completely in the dark, but its' all over now. Do you hear, they're refusing your Schnapps, says Tomaschowski, jumping to his feet. And Kossakowski shouts, from his seat: Out with the whole lousy lot! And likewise stands up and starts marching to the musicians and holds forth: We'll see who orders who around.

Now, my grandfather is also on the march, pulling along old Fagin, who is hanging on his coat-tails.

And Adam? He has furtively retired. With Gustav from Malken as it happens. They had something to discuss. And suddenly disappeared.

So now the National Defence Struggle, so familiar in German history, can begin, or rather, flare up.

Give it him. Those are Willuhn's words.

Korrinth and Nieswandt get up cautiously and quickly assess the distances and occupy the strategically vital positions: one in front of the music, the other in the centre of the triangle stove—bench—door.

Amen, says Feller, now he is at a loss. He turns away. Although that doesn't help. What the eyes don't see, the ears will hear.

Give it him and again hohohoho we shall see but not you you confounded pig.

And now advancing steps on two or three sides.

And now a groan.

A stamping, like the start of a jump.

Hohohoho.

And now the door opens. Everybody happy!

Feyerabend and Froese the knacker, to judge by the voices. Summer-fair, yes?

And there, through all the noise, a thin tenor: Very strange happenings once took place. And three, four loud voices: Hei hei hei hei.

And one very surprised one: Well really, what ever next.

There it is, and again: Give it him, and again, hohohoho. The gnashing is from grandfather's teeth.

And the crashing is from someone's footwear.

One flat hand.

Others, more like fists now.

Hohohoho.

Now the door is flung open again, this time from inside.

And Korrinth's calm instruction: Pass him over.

There goes one flying down the stairs.

Uij Uij.

Weiszmantel calls cheerily out of the window.

Pull yourself together again.

There goes the second.

Uij Uij Uij.

And another, and another. Probably Barkowski and Koschorrek to judge by the shouts. Or Ragolski.

This won't do at all.

Followed by: Get out of here, wife.

That was Rosinke.

Now one from Linde is going flying, kicking for all his worth. Keep it up, says Korrinth.

The one who is just sailing out with frightful oaths, we know only too well. And know what to expect.

He lands on his behind, supports himself with his left hand, props himself up in a sitting position, and as he recognises the man standing in front of him, roars: What are you dozing about here for, man!

Constable Adam raises two fingers to his helmet. I know my instructions.

Inside Fenske and Fagin are still sitting by the stove. They have hardly noticed a thing.

You two, says Nieswandt, fetch us a cart to drive away in. But a German one, mind.

Feller crawls out from under the bench, slips past Korrinth unnoticed, but turns round quickly in the doorway to say: You'll be hearing more about this.

I'll kick your arse, says Korrinth, but stays where he is. Not worth it. Would be too late anyway. Feller has disappeared. What Rosinke is just muttering about Chasing-Away-Best-Customers, is not true at all, and he knows it. When they have money to spend, these best customers, then off to the German House in Briesen, where all roads lead, or at least in Gollub.

And Rosine says: Give it to me a moment. Willuhn's sleeve is coming adrift from his jacket. But it's only the thread,

Rosine will fix it in a trice.

There stands Habedank, whom we haven't mentioned, but who, quite inconspicuously in our opinion, led the entire operation.

Willuhn must realise, he points to our friend Habedank and says: Scipio on the ruins of Carthage.

Ruins! Let's look around! The tables are standing, not a single chair is broken, not even a glass. Neat work, just as it should be.

And something quite new in Neumühl.

Weiszmantel stands at the window, he knows. He looks at Johann Vladimir Geethe and this flutist from Hoheneck puts it into words, with great dignity of course.

Something quite new. And we, confound it, can say we were bloody well there, damn it all. *Do stu piorunow!*

CHAPTER FOURTEEN

How much do we really know?

That people go for walks, in the wood or by the river, towards evening time, that they are together, and build walls around themselves and set a roof over their heads, are fruitful and multiply and get old in the process.

This much we know. And that there is a lot more besides, some things which are to be expected, but many which find us totally unprepared, as, for example, the incidents we are relating here. At least these few things which are to be expected, could be the same in Posen or Löbau, in Lautenburg and Ciborz and Neumühl and down towards Rozan. But is that the case? Maybe Levin, who knew his way around, has forgotten it during his year here in the Culmerland. There's this Marie, she knew it all too and keeps on forgetting. Levin comes and says Marje. No one asks where Levin was, yesterday, the day before yesterday. No one asks so many questions. Marie says: Come, let's be gone.

And so they leave Feyerabend's cottage on the site, pause a moment by the little stick-fence and say: Be seeing you, to whom then?

Then Feyerabend calls out of the door: Where are you heading for?

And Levin replies: I'll follow my nose.

Will you be back?

No.

There they go, Leo Levin and Marie Habedank.

Feyerabend calls after them: And the stones, are you leaving them here?

Yes they are leaving the stones. And the rest of the mill-jetty. That's all there is. Are they supposed to take stones with them? Mill-stones?

In his autobiography Maimon tells a story of a grandfather who was a tenant farmer, under Prince Radziwill and was responsible for a river-crossing, a couple of paths and a road in his area. When the prince's men came, governors and lords, maybe even the prince himself, and got stuck in the mud, with horses sinking in, carriages toppling and wheels breaking, then they sent for the tenant farmer and his men and horse-whipped them till they couldn't move. Then his grandfather set up a guard post by the bridge, someone had to be there all the time and sound the alarm when the Radziwill men were coming. Then they would all take refuge in the woods.

No Radziwills come riding up like that now, although the Radziwills are still in existence, and lords and governors too, and if one were to come, the tenant would stay at home, nowadays he will only run away before the Czar's Cossacks, if he can, and later, he builds himself another house as there is never anything but ashes after they have gone. But the roads and the plank-bridges are just as they were in those days. Every one of these bridges, every road is enough to infuriate Levin. There they go along the road to Grudusk, here the two, three bridges are slightly better, the road too, but what has he already put behind him, this Levin! How long have they been under way now?

They come to Tschernize Borowe, to Choynowo, to Obrembiec. A Levin has plenty of relations. Who offer a greeting with one hand and a Schnapps with the other. First they ask, then they tell stories till far into the night, once they have closed shutters, that is. Bad times.

The count at Ciborz, they say, slaughtered seven horses because they were sent back by the remounting commission. Clever man, the count, the accursed goy, one blow between the eyes and it's all over.

As though that meant something.

They say that the fellow from Gronach wants a divorce and no one will give him horses to go to the Rabbi at Czerniatyn, and they laugh. So what?

Your Uncle Schachne has built a swing, you never saw such a thing, a whole frame-work of wood, and put it in front of his house, wrapped himself in a fur scarf and plaited his beard. Sits in this swing every day and sings little songs. And Aunt Henje walks round and round the thing talking to him like a Ukrainian.

That's bad, he made money, in years gone by, and now he is supposed to be dotty.

And Berkowitz lost everything he had in a fire last year.

And you? You're going to your own people. And who's that you're going round with?

A furtive question behind the door.

Thus Marie and Levin travel on to Rozan.

A long journey. What doesn't happen during this time?

Mr. President requests Mr. Councillor to the Governor for a report, affair Neumühl.

Immediately, says Herr von Tittlack. And repeats: Affair Neumühl.

Enough, Tittlack, says Governor-President von Bahr-Uckley, simply this: necessary to restore order in Briesen.

Excellency is commanding a commission?

Tittlack! Excellency grunts, Police!

So this District President von Drießler, this Austrian, could have done that on his own initiative, but naturally: lets the whole affair drag on, sends in a report to Marienwerder, awaits instructions.

In consideration of the significance of the occurrence.

Allow me, Your Excellency.

Right, Tittlack, and would you say, Tittlack, that it is right that our border land here should have to suffer incompetent servants of the state, Tittlack, and become, as it were, an exile ground for throw-outs?

Here, of course, Tittlack replies with: Under no circumstances! and Excellency! And also enquiries regarding the additional decree regarding the regulations of October 1st 1863 concerning foreign nationalities.

Fiddlesticks, exclaims Excellency, decree, regulations—we need immigration laws. But quickly!

Yes, the immigration laws. At the moment being prepared in Berlin, and under no circumstances can they become valid as quickly as they are required. Although prominent experts are dealing with the matter: von Dragulski-Borchert, von Wojciechowski-Mehne, von Wnuk-Kostka, von Kuhlke-Kulesza and von Szwab.

But it will be there, this much has already leaked out. No more Polacks in German villages, all this confusion has got to stop.

I tell you, Tittlack, it'll come, Tittlack, as sure as Amen in church.

To which Tittlack replies, Excellency, we await the day.

Then von Bahr-Uckley says: And after that we'll take a look at the old trade-regulations.

And von Tittlack: Then these Liberals will get a surprise, it'll be their turn: artists and gypsies and professors, most amusing.

Surely not gypsies, Tittlack, but maybe you're right?

Music of the future.

He leans back, drums his toes a little. That's one more thing settled.

Councillor to the Governor von Tittlack goes to the door.

Just a moment, Tittlack, says Excellency, decoration, here take it with you.

So Glinski receives his decoration, we know what for: Exceptional loyalty. Just the superintendency of Schönsee is still outstanding. That will come his way: now that he's been decorated.

And something comes to Neumühl too: a garrison, as it were.

Exactly a week after the Neumühl summer-fair, early Monday morning, chief cavalry sergeant Plontke moves in with four police officers, and immediately takes up quarters at the scene of the disturbance, in Rosinke's tavern and hotel.

And then what?

They sit around and talk and stretch out their legs under the table. At first people come to have a look. But the blockheads sit there, talk and do nothing and have great long moustaches. No woman, they think, could fail to notice something like that. Then the people go away again. And pass the word around: Nothing doing with that lot.

As though it were nothing at all: On Tuesday two of them stay behind in Rosinke's bar-parlour with Adam, whom they called in, and three walk through the village and go in to see Germann and stay a couple of hours.

They have already been at my grandfather's.

My grandfather knows the world, Thorn, Graudenz, Marien-werder, and he knows straight away when the fellows appear in his courtyard: That is the German Empire, in shining armour, summoned to the defence of German Honour, which, as we know—is the honour of my grandfather.

Without further ado my grandfather immediately turns the conversation to Polish workers and Polish elements in general. But the German Honour has its sights set higher, Plontke's instructions are: Stop any disturbance in Neumühl and surrounding area, with help of Constable Adam.

Not that my grandfather would doubt this German Honour, not for a minute, he knows that in the case of these policemen it's all to do with matters of secondary importance, the lower ranks, that's all.

What are you getting so excited about, asks Plontke.

That's for higher places to decide, says my grandfather meaningfully, only pours out two glasses of Schnapps per person, rises to his feet and says: I have work to do, gentlemen, and I am sure other duties await you.

So they stay rather longer with Germann, four good hours, as is remarked in the village and reported by Feller to my grandfather, and they even come again the next day. They enjoy themselves with Germann.

Yes, says my grandfather, but now he doesn't believe his own words, it's more an act of self-esteem. Those fellows, he says, have got their wits about them, they're smelling out the Polacks.

Be as wise as the serpents, says Feller.

Indeed, says my grandfather.

And harmless as the dove.

But of course.

So now these uniformed serpents and doves are smelling out the Polish farmer Germann and his wife and the likewise German farmer Lebrecht and his wife who have ventured over a little through the garden gate.

Chief cavalry sergeant Plontke used to hold office in Guttstadt, then in Stuhm and for the last three years he has been stationed at Briesen. He gives short, concise descriptions of these three towns and each time mentions: garrison shooting range, practice square, disciplinary centre, or military detention centre and German House.

After a few Schnapps this fundamentally correct picture takes on a more individual character.

In Anno Kruck, or to be more exact 1807, although it doesn't really matter, a certain Napoleon ate up the last cow in all Guttstadt there. That's history for you.

In Stuhm, when you take a walk with a lady, by the lake at dusk, there are such huge gnats, they sting your bare behind. This refers to relationships with the civilian population. Every day in Briesen you see the same drunkards in the gutter, each one has his particular time, this one-time cavalry captain at nine, secretary Bonikowski at ten, notary Willutzki at eleven, you can put your clock right by them. So those are the official duties.

I know a precious shiny stone, the German policemen sing and they mean the German heart, that well-known shiny precious stone, in the words of the bard, as bright as the day and noble, of course.

Damned jolly folk, these Polacks. And so German. We'll go there again soon, and you're rolling drunk, Plontke rebukes his commando, pull yourselves together, you are wearing the Emperor's coat.

They've arrived. Levin stops over the Narew, on the green slope. Over on the lower bank lies the town. Only the post office is here on the high bank, under the four trees, as before, they've not even grown any taller. In these eighteen months, in this long, long, time.

Over there is the town. The two towers. The stone buildings around them. Thrust towards the river by the cluster of wooden houses, so that the reed roofs are compressed together, and for their part the little houses send out tiny wooden huts and covered jetties in to the murky waters of the Narew.

The water comes and allows itself to be stopped and led aside, it flows on with slow whirling motions, carrying with it thin strips of foam, which, from up here, look like Weiszmantel-type wreaths of white clover, it rips and plucks them asunder, swallows them up and they disappear.

There are the tanneries, says Levin, my people live there.

Shall I come with you, Marie asks.

Its got to be.

Come, says Levin.

The house, where Levin's people live, is very old. The door is framed by two stone pillars which support a round arch. The arch is older than the house, it's supposed to have come from the Orient, someone is supposed to have brought it back, so they say, but it's probably not true. The door is heavy and the iron hinges creak.

Inside the dark room, now penetrated by a wide shaft of daylight, an old grey dog has curled up to sleep on a sack, it only lifts its head as Levin enters and stands in the shaft of light, a dark figure.

Go back to sleep, says Levin and the little dog pokes its nose into its fur.

First he runs off and now he's back, say Levin's people, but kindly and without asking any questions, Leo will talk when he feels like it. Or they'd really have to ask about this girl too. But Levin will tell them everything in good time.

Levin helps in the tanneries for a couple of days, Marie too. The day after the Sabbath Levin says: You haven't asked any questions and I haven't given any answers, so now I say, we're moving on, there's nothing to stay here for, for us.

Aunt Perel says: But children, you can stay. Well what shall they do, go or stay?

Levin bows before the Father. The Father lays his hands upon him, he says: Go.

Levin steps out from under the archway. Marje.

And Marie says: Come.

There they go. Uncle Dowid, the teacher, is drawing signs on the floorboards with his stick. No one will read them. He sits in the house, old, and lifts up his face. In this world, he says, the laws wander around and stand in our rooms and have wide eyes and long ears and say: There shall be parting and no union.

Aunt Perel sits on the bench, face buried in hands, rocking backwards and forwards. And Uncle Dowid continues: In the other world we shall see those who have parted, they'll be standing together, their arms around each other.

In the other world, says Uncle Dowid.

Not our world. Farewell Marie. Farewell Levin.

Tomorrow Marie will be talking as Jan Marcin has always talked, of things of yesterday and yesteryear. But that was a long time ago, sweetheart, all that decays as quickly as your teeth.

But as you say it, hold your Levin by the hand.

Neumühl, that was a long time ago. Tell him that.

Now the limes are blossoming in front of Rosinke's tavern.

Where the policemen are still hanging around. Plontke is writing his second report.

The first one read: Arrived, taken up quarters, everyone well. In the second chief cavalry sergeant Plontke turns his attention to the situation in hand.

And the company at Briesen receive the following script:

The atmosphere is very good, the civilian population is pursuing its normal occupation, the Poles, God forbid, have no thoughts of causing trouble.

Only my grandfather, according to the report, is persisting in a stubborn attitude and obstinately dissenting with the instructed instructions.

Abstinently dispensing were chief cavalry sergeant Plontke's actual words and what he is referring to with these supposed instructions, we don't know either. But how do you express yourself to give the police authorities in Briesen a picture that suits them? Do we know that any better than Plontke? Who has his experience, from Guttstadt and Stuhm. We'll let him write something, which looks good, on paper.

Plontke, required by Briesen to express himself more clearly concerning the obstinacy of my grandfather, replies: the said mill-owner, disdainful of the Emperor's coat, was inciting the peaceable population.

Well, well, the gentlemen say. An enquiry arrives for Chief Administrator Nolte which the sick man has sent over to my grandfather, just as it stands, on the headed paper. Best wishes. Johann might like to take a look.

Shall I take some message or other, asks Nolte's landlady. She delivered the note.

No, says my grandfather, not necessary.

Now she can go again, prefers to stay a while with Aunt Wife. Christina, my little one, they surely don't want anything from you now, do they?

No, says Christina, what could they possibly want?

My grandfather comes in to the kitchen. He says to the old woman: You go home now. And to Christina: You come along in. Tomorrow I'm going to Briesen.

There he sits adjusting his dark countenance.

Sort things out a bit. Who do they think they are?

No, a voice like Konopka at midnight.

But here we've added another sentence to our list: Number twenty-five.

Do you think it's necessary, asks Aunt Wife.

Necessary is maybe a little too strong. Let's just say: It can't do any harm.

Prepare the supper then, grandfather says, here comes Feller. He's got a nose like Diewelinski's hound!

Dear Christina, says Feller.

People are so friendly when they're curious.

But we'll say to Feller: You be quiet and wait. My grandfather will tell you as much as is good for you.

Sit down, he says.

And they sit. My grandfather dourly saws away at the bacon and salts the already salty stuff again from sheer depression. You're quite cunning for a preacher, he thinks, I'll surprise you yet.

He, my grandfather, is a man of lone decisions. So he only tells Brother Feller what he has already revealed to Aunt Wife: Tomorrow I'm going to Briesen.

And Feller thinks: Still that business with the mill. And he says: The Jew Levin has gone, Feyerabend thinks it's for good. Says he heard it from Levin himself.

Well then, says my grandfather, but he can't stop his mouth suddenly working faster, well then, he's gone, layabout, eternally loafing around here, what was he after, there was nothing more to be gained for him by staying.

And Feller thinks: You can talk, if the right people had testified, there would have been plenty to be gained: for the Jew.

Well just tell them what's what in Briesen, says Feller firmly

212

piling high his plate, then the whole business will be over and forgotten. And he thinks: Silly of Levin really, I wouldn't have allowed the old boy to treat me like that.

Briesen, says my grandfather, that's the place, when I'm old, I'm going to move to Briesen.

What, cries Christina anxiously. What do you want in Briesen?

Then grandfather becomes more cheerful, wipes his mouth and says: Perhaps you think I am old, well you can just think again.

Come, come, says Feller, man in the prime of life. And turning to Aunt Wife: Where he's right, he's right. Briesen is an excellent town, when I get old, I don't know. Stop it now, you two, says Christina, that's enough of your Briesen, Briesen.

The old boy, well yes, he does say such things from time to time, but Feller, the pious Brother, he should hold his peace: Briesen!

And yet, Christina, you don't even know what Feller knows: What the drunken cavalry captain revealed: Women like grains of sand by the sea.

How often have you been to Briesen then, asks Christina.

Used to go a lot, says my grandfather. When the mill was being built. König delivered everything, a fine firm, when it was all there and unloaded, he stood beers all round.

Do you know, says Feller, it's very pretty in Briesen. Just like a picture. You sit at the window, there's the market place, big houses, the Protestants' spire. There's a chapel there too, at the other end, but not too far away, with a proper baptistry with steps going down on either side.

So you said before, says Christina.

It's possible of course, to go on and on about Briesen.

Where all roads lead.

At any rate tomorrow my grandfather is driving to Briesen.
We'll go to bed now, tomorrow will be a long day.
This night my grandfather dreams that he's walking through
a completely strange house.
Black beams, unhewn, iron hooks in the walls, from which
pinewood lamps project at angles into the dark rooms; biting
air. Faceless people wander around, no one speaks. Not a
sound. When he approaches one of the figures it vanishes.
And he stops still and says: Good day. And hears the sound
of his own voice, as though he had never heard it before, a
shrill voice. On the bench by the wall, from out of the
animal skins, a figure emerges, the entire face grown over
with long white hair, with huge eyes, in which the reflection
of a fire flickers. Jastrzemb. He's saying something about
hawks. He lifts up a silver horse-shoe, he nestles a cross in
front of his breast, a bluish light spreads over the wall behind
him, flies upward and covers the ceiling like a heaven, and
now from outside crying, a hundred voices, in the opening
door is the fire.
Today, that's the shrill voice again.
He sees himself step across the threshold, he hears this today,
soaring above the hundred voices, he raises his hand, stillness,
the fire is petrified.
A grey mass, riders and carts. All passing him by.
At the gate women and children. The courtyard stays behind.
Now the woods open up. Above the blackness first light
appears. The stars are still there, trembling, in the ice.
Cold, says my grandfather.
With this word he begins the day.
He gets up. Christina is already bustling around in the
kitchen. As if distracted, he stands in the doorway. Husband,
what is it? He waves aside her question. Three, four words
this morning. Good-bye. And so he leaves. For Briesen.

Christina has stowed everything under the seat for him, coffee, home-made beer, elderberry juice. What's got into him again? With that she goes back inside the house.

What could it be? A long time ago, one man left his house and never came back. My grandfather recognised him immediately, Poleske.

There he sits, on his cart, my grandfather. Thats' the way it was, for sure, he never came back. Then he lifts the whip, draws it once to the left and once to the right across the horses' backs, makes himself comfortable again, says: That's enough. And so, without turning a hair he comes through this dream, this

VISION NUMBER FIVE

In Briesen everything goes like clockwork. My grandfather says not a word about the little stamped paper, that Nolte sent him, simply mentioning, but in the right quarters, that he happens to be here, on business, but that this certain Levin recently disappeared, some foggy night, to Congress-Poland.

Where he belongs, is the comment of the gentlemen at Briesen.

Nebenzahl closes the files. Chief cavalry sergeant Plontke's third report has also arrived. Which emphatically repeats that the Poles are extremely German. But also confirms: One certain Levin has gone away, together with one certain Marie, daughter of the local horse-gypsy and musician Habedank. Over the green border, as they say, although it's actually a river. But as everyone knows the Drewenz is just as green, if not, particularly now, greener than the meadows, which accompany it.

Then my grandfather, this man of lone decisions, has a few

more things to attend to. Which leads him to pay a visit the next day to the offices of Königs' saw-mills and box-making factory. The one-time junior has turned in to a stout fellow with a full beard and rounded movements, scarcely recognisable.

In the afternoon my grandfather sits in Wiezorrek's German House with Schwill the broker. Schwill takes a piece of paper from his jacket pocket, but it's all so simple that he doesn't need to note anything down.

Yes, and on the third day my grandfather is back in Neumühl. By the evening.

He stands in the moonlight in the courtyard. Shuts all the doors himself, bolts the gate.

He comes indoors. We're moving to Briesen.

Aunt Wife drops the dish of bilberries on the stone floor. Fragments of china scattered here. Berries scattered there. Reddish-blue-tinged milk flows over the floor.

CHAPTER FIFTEEN

Hey there, calls Philippi the painter and runs across the entire square, arms outstretched, leaps over the gutter with a single bound, stands in front of my grandfather and says: And who are you, I haven't met you before.

At this my grandfather retreats half, or maybe a quarter step, just the sort of movement so to speak, backwards or in any other direction, it's difficult to say, simultaneously stretching from the waist upwards, a kind of shock pose, which certain beetles and other insects adopt in the face of unpleasant surprises, or at unexpected encounters in general, exactly that and nothing else.

So that's what he did, my grandfather, conquered the surprise, regained the dignity, nothing can happen now, now he can say, leaning lightly on his walking stick, mouth half-closed: What can I do for you, sir?

The perfect townsman, my grandfather, a credit to this den Briesen. You've got to hand it to him.

Come, come, not another word, says Philippi the painter. He has thoroughly enjoyed the whole pretty performance, now he is slightly annoyed, but really only a very little, by the contemptuous tone of voice in which my grandfather calls him Sir.

Come now, no nonsense, says Philippi. They are now right in front of Wiezorreck's German House, right in front of the door. Come, first you shall have a couple of beers.

Dreadful ale-house, quite dreadful. Philippi the painter shakes himself. He stretches out both arms in front of himself, fingers

spread wide, pulls such a disgusted face, that my grandfather has probably never seen anything like it, in the whole
of his life, a face that perhaps could only otherwise be pulled
by my grandfather himself: in other words a monstrous,
disgusted face. Fancy having to sit in such a filthy hovel.
German House. It makes you laugh.

Herr Philippi, says Wiezorreck, rushing up, wiping-up cloth
still clutched in his fingers, Herr Philippi, you won't cause
me any unpleasantness, now will you.

He utters the words in a hushed tone, almost pleading, putting two fingers in front of his mouth, but Philippi grasps
him by the coat-button and pulls him closer. My dear fellow,
says Philippi, what are you whispering for?

Wiezorreck resolves to smile, shrugs apologetically, no one
knows: for himself or for Philippi the painter, his shoulders,
says, turning to my grandfather, but also to the four or
five other guests, who are bound to know it already and
are paying no attention: Artistic temperament of course.
The gentlemen know each other?

Not a whit, says Philippi. This poor fellow has just come from
the graveyard.

But never, says my grandfather, how do you make that out?
Shut up, says Philippi, and hooks himself grandfather as
well, now he has two by their coat-buttons. Yes, and what's
that milk-and-honey face for?

What can you say to that?

Beer, calls Philippi sighing, he lets the pair of them go, throws
himself into the nearest armchair, whistles with two fingers,
beckons my grandfather who is standing there as though
confronted by a ghost.

Go on, says Wiezorrek. How did you come across him?

But who is it, asks my grandfather.

Academy painter Herwig Philippi, never heard of him?

218

Aha, an artist. And here in Briesen. Incredible. Something quite new for my grandfather.

Wiezorrek has left him standing. Here come the beers. What are you hanging about over there for, shouts Philippi the painter, come, your beer.

Our story finds itself, to a certain extent, in liquidation.

One character after another is disappearing from it, we simply let them go, or there again perhaps not so simply; yes, to be honest, in some cases, we find it quite difficult: now they are to leave, but where will they go?

But at this very point in this dismal story we are introducing a new character: this artist, and there must be a reason, the reason is: It is autumn.

Autumn. Not another word about the five or six or seven weeks of summer, in which our story has taken place so far. It is autumn. My grandfather has sold his property in Neumühl, for a very favourable price, house and land, all the livestock and the mill too, the mill now! now just before the busy milling season! To Rosinke by the way. Who now, in addition to his hotel, possesses a water-mill, the only one in Neumühl, as we know. Nieswandt and Korrinth he reinstates without delay.

So he has sold up, my grandfather. But why exactly? Is he beaten? And is he admitting it? Or is he just tired? But there's very little sense, it seems to me, in asking.

There's very little sense in asking.

That might very well be another of these sentences we keep referring to. It might, and there again, it might not. I don't mind, let it be: sentence Number twenty-six.

And why do we introduce the comic character?

We always need comic characters![1] Need them very much in fact. This one, this academy painter Philippi weighs a good

[1] Twenty-seventh sentence.

couple of hundredweight, but he carries it like nothing at all, on tiny feet he dances down the street, tells stories: My mother used to say to me, then follows something different every time, twiddles a small cane with ivory point and knob between three fingers or waves around a white card: Children and military servicemen half-price, something like that, but decorated with strewn flowers and a dense gaily painted garland of dahlias round the edge. And now he is sitting opposite my grandfather. And we need him.

My grandfather has sold up. He is now a citizen of Briesen. But how about all the money?

One day Feller arrives. Travelling with Froese the knacker. Grandfather is sitting in his best parlour reading his *Gartenlaube*. It's a good magazine, printed in Berlin, under the eyes of His Majesty. He reads and a strange feeling comes over him. There's an article, what's the name of the man who wrote it, the author? Glagau, Otto Glagau, that's his name, and this is an extremely important article, my grandfather's ears are already red when Christina enters with Brother Feller. Just look Johann, what fine visitors we have.

She is really pleased, Christina, and has a right to be, up till now she has been pre-occupied only with moving, getting straight, finding her way around, making new curtains, every day, and my grandfather is pleased too. Well it's you, he says And: Sit down. Best wishes from Neumühl, says Feller. Sits down. Wears his most meaningful expression.

Fire away, says my grandfather.

And now it comes out, point by point, exactly as Feller had planned during the long journey, firstly, secondly, thirdly. Johann, says Feller, there's this business with the congregation. You were one of our Elders.

Still am really.

Well yes, everything happened so quickly, and just at harvest time.

We thought, says Feller, the farewell party could be held later. At Christmas perhaps.

Look here now, says my grandfather, am I supposed to go all the way to Neumühl just for that, God forbid! I'll simply remain an Elder.

That's impossible Johann, you know it yourself.

Well then, beams my grandfather, you can make me an honorary Elder, they have them, Rocholl's father was one, you might remember.

I know, answers Feller grasping his collar. But then he continues bravely. But at the time, I know very well, he also paid for the entire chapel roof.

So what? What are you trying to say?

Perhaps if you were to take over the costs of the baptistry or immersion bath, it's all the same.

So that's it, money.

It's always the same story with you, says my grandfather. Just don't approach me from that angle, I tell you, that's one thing I can't bear. Baptistry or immersion bath, it's all the same, well I'm deaf on that score.

Johann, says Feller.

Not another word, commands my grandfather, haven't I done enough for you? What more do you want?

But Johann, I'm not saying anything, it's not on my account, it's the congregation, they must agree and there must be something to show for it!

You lot! says my grandfather. You're never satisfied! And pulls a face very similar to the recent disgusted one of the painter Philippi, externally: the eyelids half closed, the brows raised, particularly towards the temples, the corners of his mouth drooping, a verticle furrow divides the brow. You lot!

And as Feller remains silent: Go on, what else?

Johann, says Feller, your daughter Lene has written to me. To me too, says my grandfather.

Well then you know. Feller is relieved. But not for long. My grandfather spares him nothing. No, no, you tell me. Well Lene in Dortmund, married to a master brewer there has written: What about the money? Now that father has sold up. And after all a share was entered in her name.

She can just stop pushing her luck, the young hussey, big dowry and then more in cash and her old man earns good money. My grandfather is beginning to feel uncomfortable. And now she hides behind you, Alwin and you allow yourself to be influenced, of course. I think, Alwin, you might very well write her something concerning the fourth commandment. Which is, by the way, the only commandment which promises: In order that it may go well with thee and thy days may be lengthened.

Johann, says Feller.

But of course, I know, you're all the same, take, take, take. My grandfather begins to feel hot, he runs to the window and flings open both shutters. There he stands and would dearly love to shout down to the market: That's how your children turn out, that's what you've brought up!

Calm yourself, Johann, says Feller.

Go on, says my grandfather closing the window. Your son Gerhard has written to me of course.

He would too cried my grandfather.

Who else?

Albert and Frieda.

Aunt Wife coffee, says my grandfather, shaken. And after he has lowered himself into a chair: That only leaves Erwin.

No, not him, says Feller, he wouldn't accept anything from you.

Coffee!

That's the way it is, now that my grandfather is in Briesen. He needs a comic character.

Are you angry then, the comic character asks. Anger makes you ugly.

Let's have a beer, says my grandfather.

He sits here often now, in Wiezorrek's German House. Once the comic character, this Academy artist, dragged him to a very different tavern, one with two women. Quite nice there, although my grandfather was expecting something else. There was only beer.

But now my grandfather is sitting at home, in his best parlour. This article, this *Gartenlaube* article, by this gentleman or author Glagau, Otto. There it is: No longer may tolerance or miserable weakness prevent us Christians from taking preventative measures against the extravagances, excesses and affrontery of the Jewry.

Aunt Wife, come here and listen to this.

Jewry. No longer may we suffer the Jews to thrust themselves to the foreground in every sphere. They are constantly trampling on us Christians—there you have it—they are pushing us to the wall, they are usurping our very air and breath.

Now listen to that: in Berlin too!

Why? Christina is confused. What's he getting at?

Exactly the same as here, explains my grandfather. If you think of this pikestaff Levin.

And now my grandfather hits upon a very happy phrase and says it slowly, word for word: In Berlin, it seems to me, they're not man enough .

Deeply and audibly he breathes in and then adds: Under the eyes of His Majesty and don't know what to do!

So my grandfather writes, as a Man and a German, a letter. To the author, this Herr Glagau, Otto Glagau, highly esteemed, care of the *Gartenlaube* in Berlin.

Firstly a lengthy dissertation, but then: And herewith challenge you to solve the problem without delay in the light of my example.

Signature. Underneath: Resident of Briesen, of independent means, ex mill-owner, honorary elder of the Neumühl community.

But that's not true, says Aunt Wife.

You'll see, says my grandfather (Twenty-eighth sentence).

This evening, in Wiezorrek's tap-room, Philippi the painter says: I know you, you're in a good mood today, you've pulled off something.

And as my grandfather relates what he has written to Berlin today, to this *Gartenlaube* in Berlin, to this author, Philippi springs to his feet and spits on the table. And I've drunk beer with someone like this, devil take you!

And he's gone.

Funny chap. Was getting to be a nuisance. It's better this way. But my grandfather cannot avoid running into this painter from time to time in Briesen. That is not so pleasant. For this fat fellow proceeds to mince a wide circle round my grandfather, taps himself on the forehead, grabs a lock of his long hair, pulls it upwards, clasps himself on the behind with his other hand and whistles a silly tune, spinning round to it, finally sticks out his tongue and then suddenly stands there with drooping arms and sad face, turns on his heel and runs away.

Does this mean that there is someone here who has not given up my grandfather? He hardly knows him. Funny fellow! Well, artists. What goes on inside their heads. In such artists' heads.

But those must be two sentences, twenty-nine and thirty. Events are really moving a little too quickly at the moment. Now that we are reaching the end.

Philippi, the painter, sits outside the little town, towards evening, by the smaller of the two lakes, over yonder the Falkenau meadows begin. He has a piece of paper in front of him and is writing on it instead of drawing:

> Herb, yellow, vault
> Of lips at midday,
> Dry waters
> Scents, mist and once
> Snow,
> I speak into the wind.

Good fellow, this Philippi. Keeps himself to himself, can't talk to anyone, at least not to people, although he talks a lot, about this and that, says to the mayor Good customer and to the chief of Police: Mind how you look. Nobody understands what he is trying to say when he talks like that. He looks at his trousers. How nice it is to have trousers, you don't go around with such bare legs.

A good painter too.

Here he comes, back to the town, along the lower castle street, wearing his *Kalabreser*—a tiny little hat. And meets my grandfather. But he is not in the mood for dancing.

And my grandfather sees no opportunity of avoiding this painter without undignified haste, so he pulls himself together and says, rather too loudly: I see Sir, that you appear to be taking the air.

Quite right, says Philippi, does you good, you should try it.

I should? but why? My grandfather is not so much annoyed as astonished. How do you mean?

I'll explain some time.

Philippi is tired. When my grandfather tries to join him, he waves him away. Tomorrow.

Well clear off then, thinks my grandfather, I shan't force my company on you.

Although it might be better, for my grandfather, if he were to force his company, really force himself upon this artist. For he can't try it on us any more, we have given him up. This painter who's always running around here, says my grandfather.

He is sitting with cavalry captain von Lojewski, in the German House.

Oh him, says this cavalry captain, quite a cultured fellow, in some ways. Painted the altar-pieces here, both of them, Protestant and Catholic, doesn't happen often. Excellent I tell you, you ought to take a look, painted from live models, I have the honour of knowing the ladies.

The reference is to the two Marys and Mary and Martha, that is: their originals, the present Frau Thulewitz and Fräulein von Binkowski in the Home for Gentlewomen, the widowed Frau Schulz in Trutenau and Frau Myszkowski, wife of the Forestry Commissioner now in Marienwerder. Lojewski can talk, he has never had his ears boxed by Philippi, he doesn't use force. He doesn't get beer from him either, hasn't for a long time.

Lojewski has a similar problem with this artist to my grandfather.

With him it's on account of the Poles. Cultured fellow, this Philippi, but very odd views, pity really.

When you're stuck here in the provinces, says Lojewski, it does you good in some ways to meet a cultured person.

Well you can have beer from me too, snaps grandfather; what's this fellow saying about provinces. Briesen—provincial! But this is too much for a nobleman!

Kindly alter your tone of voice, says the cavalry captain, you've never been in the army, I suppose?

This costs my grandfather at least six beers and three liqueurs too. And those are the people you mix with, grandfather. But it's all the same to us.

As all roads lead to Briesen, so too do all roads leads away from Briesen. The one that goes to Neumühl, via Falkenau, Polkau, Linde, Garczewo, across the stretch of railway, over the little Struga river, along the reed ponds, we've already walked and ridden this road. Now we come this way for the last time. In the autumn. The fields are empty. All is still over the waters. The birds congregate around the deadwood. The air is damp and smells bitter.

There lies Neumühl. And Neumühl too is still. The policemen, Plontke and the four other moustaches have left. Rosinke leans against the shop door, mill-owner now, but he won't give up the tavern. He says to constable Adam who is standing behind him: You can have a good life here. You can grow old here. The last one was always prying around too much, no one likes that.

We shall see, says Adam cautiously.

What do you mean: see? Adam has already gained experience in this short time: Always keep out of everything, everywhere, simply don't be there, that's the fruit of his experience. And everything really did disappear in the sand, just disappeared into the sand, and it all looked so dangerous at first. This Union of Malken and the whole Neumühl affair, first in the circus and then in Rosinke's tavern. At any rate that's the way it seems. But Adam won't get old here, at any rate not with these tactics.

But now Neumühl is quiet. The Germans and the pious folk were totally confused by the departure of my grandfather and most of all by its obvious lack of justification. And the others?

Lebrecht and Germann are, according to official confirmation, pro-German, although they may not always have been so. Nieswandt and Korrinth can provide proof of employment again and so no one can harm them. For Feyerabend, for Olga Wendehold, for Fenske from Sadlinken, the personification of unrest, in other words my grandfather, has gone, but they still talk about him.

Aunt Huse hears news of him too. He has after all moved nearer to her. But that doesn't trouble her. She'll pay him a visit one day.

And the others, there were more, weren't there.

Habedank says: Where might Marie be now?

Last week Geethe returned from Hoheneck, he had dissolved his business there and heard that the pair of them were said to be in Ciechanow. Someone told him, someone who ought to know a Ratzkecatcher, a gypsy who makes rat- and mouse-traps from wire and mends pots and pans.

Bound to be right, says Jan Marcin, they work hard. It's not clear whether he means Levin and Marie or these rat catcher fellows who appear all over the place.

The whole company has assembled in Jan Marcin's cottage. And it's packed full, the coloured cockerel is greeting his lady-friend Francesca and Jan Marcin is happy: the little children are there. The Italian Circus have moved in. Next week another guest performance in Gollub. And in Gollub the new circus people will appear: Habedank, Geethe, Willuhn.

Music, music and more music.

Only Weiszmantel doesn't join in.

No, my little ones, says Weiszmantel, you sing, you can all sing much better. He is holding Jan Marcin's cat in his lap, tickling him behind his ears and on his forehead where such an animal can't possibly lick itself. No, my little ones, I shall move on, we'll meet again.

And so he leaves, old Weiszmantel. He will sing, there and there, everywhere he finds injustice and there's more than enough of that, so he will find more than enough to sing. Sometimes you don't see it right away, because the devil is covering it with his tail. He'll look in on the curate in Strasburg, this Weiszmantel and they'll chat away the evening together. And finally curate Rogalla will say: what devil ever rode me that I crept into this hole.

And Weiszmantel will answer: Devil or no devil, you stay here, better you than some other.

And curate Rogalla will know: That's a gift of Weiszmantel's. Says what everyone else is thinking. As a farewell the curate says: God will protect you, and: Come again, Herr Weiszmantel. It is autumn. And Weiszmantel wants to go to Löbau. Not directly, more by way of the villages, so not via Neumark and Samplau, more to the east via Gwistzyn and Tinnewalde, he has a brother in Zlottowo, and that's where he's heading, but there's plenty of time, till winter.

He's still singing. Now, in the autumn.

Something did indeed happen which never happened before. Not this old here-Poles-here-Germans or here-Christians-here Heathens, something quite different, we were there to see it, how we talk of it still. It all happened and so it can't be done away with. Weiszmantel will sing about it. And God will protect him. The way Weiszmantel does it will, I think, meet with His approval.

There he goes, the rags round his legs are tied across his loins with strings, Weiszmantel who knows songs and swings his left arm a little. We lean on the fence and watch him go, till it gets dark. There he goes, far in the distance.

And now I just wonder if it wouldn't have been better to set the whole story more to the north or still better much further to the north east, in Lithuania, where I know the whole area, rather than here, where I have never been on this Drewenz river, on the Neumühl stream, on the Struga brook, which I only know from hearsay.

But why? The story could have taken place in so many towns and in so many districts, and it was only intended to be narrated here. In thirty four sentences. So there are still four to come. Here they are:

Come, let us sing.

In Gollub the gypsies are playing.

If we don't sing, others will.

One more sentence remains. Philippi, the painter, comes running with a little skip over the gutter, and stands arms outstretched:

Now, must I explain something to you.

My grandfather replies: Not that I know of. And takes a step backwards. And says, with a hesitant glance: Leave me in peace.

No, cries Philippi the painter, spins like a top on his heel, and claps his hands, just in front of my grandfather's nose. As though he had caught a fly.

And we'll count this Philippian No. As our final sentence.

New Directions Paperbooks—A Partial Listing

For complete listing request free catalog from
New Directions, 80 Eighth Avenue, New York 10011

†Bilingual

For complete listing request free catalog from
New Directions, 80 Eighth Avenue, New York 10011   †Bilingual